# Confessions of a Gangsta 3

Nicholas Lock

Lock Down Publications & Ca$h
Presents
# Confessions of a Gangsta 3
A Novel by *Nicholas Lock*

Nicholas Lock

# Lock Down Publications

P.O. Box 944

Stockbridge, Ga 30281

Visit our website at www.lockdownpublications.com

Cover design and layout by: **Dynasty's Cover Me**
Book interior design by: **Shawn Walker**
Edited by: **Jill Duska**

## Stay Connected with Us!

Text **LOCKDOWN** to 22828 to stay up-to-date with new releases, sneak peaks, contests and more...

**Thanks**

# Submission Guideline

Submit the first three chapters of your completed manuscript to ldpsubmissions@gmail.com, subject line: Your book's title. The manuscript must be in a .doc file and sent as an attachment. Document should be in Times New Roman, double spaced and in size 12 font. Also, provide your synopsis and full contact information. If sending multiple submissions, they must each be in a separate email.

Have a story but no way to send it electronically? You can still submit to LDP/Ca$h Presents. Send in the first three chapters, written or typed, of your completed manuscript to:

LDP: Submissions Dept
Po Box 944
Stockbridge, Ga 30281

*DO NOT send original manuscript. Must be a duplicate. *

Provide your synopsis and a cover letter containing your full contact information.

Thanks for considering LDP and Ca$h Presents.

## Shout Outs

The first shout out goes to the man upstairs. Without him, there's no me or *Confessions of a Gangsta.*

Mama! You already know I love you. It's me and you against the world.

Coco and Aniyah, Daddy loves y'all to the moon and back!

To my niggas, my real homeboys. Y'all know who y'all is, the ones who haven't forgot about ya boi for these past eleven years. When I touch the streets, I'm going to the top and I'm going to bring y'all with me.

Tashae, I love you, li'l sis.

To all the family... I love you, even the ones who seem to have forgotten about Nick. Guess it's true, outta sight, outta mind.

Fayetteville, North Carolina, stand up! We here for the long haul, AANANT!

I gotta shout Cash and the whole LDP staff for the opportunity to put my thoughts on paper for the world to read.

I gotta give the fans love. I'm going to have to set up a page or an address so we can interact and I can have y'all's input on the books.

Nicholas Lock

# Chapter 1

"Meosha, push that damn baby out and quit playing," Kiki said.

Kiki was in the delivery room with Meosha as she had D'Angel. It had been two months since Bella had come to Kiki with her dad's head in a box. They had joined forces and had for the most part taken control of the U. S. underworld. Everything went through them, from drugs to guns. With the Cartel's resources and manpower and Kiki's brain, they were an unstoppable force.

"Here she comes!" a nurse said.

D'Angel came out pitch black like Meosha, but instead of having her mother's grey eyes, hers were a light silver color. They were almost white. The doctor slapped her on the ass, trying to get her to cry, but she only looked at him. He drew his hand back to pop her again, but Kiki caught his hand.

"Don't hit her anymore. She's good."

The doctor looked at Kiki, saw the look on her face and the grip on his hand. He handed D'Angel off to the nurses to get cleaned up while he stitched Meosha up

"Look at my baby!" Meosha cried when they handed her D'Angel.

D'Angel immediately latched onto Meosha's breast. Kiki could see the love in Meosha's eyes as she looked down at D'Angel.

"Taz had some strong genes. All his kids look exactly like him," Meosha said, continuing to stare into D'Angel's face.

Kiki walked out of the room as tears began to well up in her eyes.

Taz's name still made her emotional. Kiki still wasn't over losing Taz, and every time she looked into her baby's face she saw Taz, which made matters worse. She felt like her life would be so much easier if Taz was still alive. She'd give anything for Taz to walk through the door right now.

Kiki had so much on her plate with running OTF and raising the twins that she was starting to feel overwhelmed. And she knew it was only going to get worse, because she had found the information that her mother had for Taz. Her mom had found out that the big dude with the dreads from Haiti was named Zeus, and he was the new leader of the Zoe Pound Mafia. Kiki knew that when she shared this information with Bella, he was going to be marked for death, and it was most likely going to be by her hands. He'd kidnapped Bella and killed Bella and Taz's son Junior, so Kiki was sure Bella wanted him for herself. She was going to wait until Bella had her daughter, then she would tell her, because if she told her now, Bella would try to hop her six month pregnant ass on the plane to Haiti.

"We're taking her back to her room," a nurse said, wheeling a sleeping Meosha out of the delivery room.

Kiki followed behind them, peeping her security team not too far from her. They put Meosha in her bed and left, leaving Kiki alone with her twin. Her security was posted up on both ends of the hallway with one standing outside the room. Kiki and Meosha each had security teams. Kiki had taken over OTF and changed the whole modus operandi. Every position of power inside the OTF had their own security detail. Kiki shared up all the weaknesses she felt OTF had. She'd learned from her mother's mistakes and she was determined not to make the same ones.

"Where's the baby?" Keishana asked, walking into the room

"She in the nursery," Kiki informed her.

Kiki and Keishana had gotten close since Taz's death. Everyone that Taz dealt with on a personal level, Kiki tried to do the same. She felt like she would be closer to Taz by doing this. It helped that Keishana was cool as a fan. She was also the unofficial babysitter too.

"Come on so I can see her," Keishana urged.

Kiki shook her head and led the way. "Stay here with my twin. I'm just going to the nursery," Kiki told the security team before bending the corner.

"Which one is she?"

"Oh, you don't know?" Kiki raised a brow.

"There she go right there," Keishana pointed. "Oh my God, is she blind?" she asked, looking at her almost white eyes. "It's amazing that all his kids look just like him," Keishana said more to herself than Kiki. "So what you been up to?"

"Nothing much, just taking care of these babies and trying to run OTF without incident."

"And how is that working out for you?" she asked, putting her back on the nursery glass and facing Kiki.

"It's stressful as hell, but I'm good. Nothing I can't handle, and besides, I knew what I was signing up for from the start."

"If Taz was here, you'd have your hands full," Keishana said, causing Kiki to smile.

Kiki knew Taz would've probably been made her take a step back from running OTF. He'd told her he was going to take the twins if she took over OTF, but she knew he was just talking to be talking.

"When you be babysitting, how do Damiyana be acting?"

"Oh, she's going to be a mean one," Keishana informed her.

"I was thinking the same thing. She's got a better mean mug than a lot of adults I know."

They walked back to Meosha's room and she was sitting up in her bed.

"Where y'all coming from?" Meosha asked groggily.

"Looking at that pretty baby you got," Keishana said.

"Thank you. What do y'all think Taz would've said about me having his baby?" Meosha asked. He had died before she could tell him.

"He wouldn't have tripped too much, especially after seeing D'Angel. You know he don't play about his little girls," Keishana said, giving Meosha some closure.

Meosha had been unsure of what Taz would've thought because they'd only had sex one time and she had tricked him into that. She had snuck into his room late one night and fucked him. The whole time, he thought she was somebody else until she revealed it to him. Meosha had tried a few times after that, but Taz always rebuffed her advances.

"Kiki, there's someone out here for you," Tevin, her security guard, peeked his head in and said.

Kiki wasn't expecting anyone, especially at the hospital. The only person it could be was Bella, Kiki thought to herself.

"What are you doing here and what do you want?" she said when she came out and saw Vinnie Two Times standing there.

Vinnie Two Times was a capo in the Italian Mafia. He and Taz had struck a deal when Taz was trying to kill Hector. Taz had been introduced to Vinnie by the son of one of his business partners. Since Hector was Taz's old plug and head of the Mexican Cartel, he needed the top notch work Vinnie had and the much-needed info he had on Hector and his whereabouts. But when Bella killed her pops and took over the Mexican Cartel, Kiki cut Vinnie off and started getting her work from Bella, and that had put a major dent in Vinnie's pockets. With the amount of money that was pouring in from dealing with Kiki, the family heads were thinking of giving him the spot of one of the dons that had fallen out of favor and was on the Feds' radar. So Vinnie had to keep Kiki on his team or else he would be relegated to capo for the rest of his life.

"Is that how you treat an old friend?" Vinnie asked.

"Old friend?" Kiki scrunched her face up. "We've never been friends, Vinnie. You and Taz were business partners; that's it. Once again, what are you doing here?"

"We have some things to discuss, particularly why you haven't been getting any coke from me."

"I thought you would've gotten the hint, but I see you haven't, so here's the deal. I got a new plug, so your services are no longer needed."

"That wasn't the agreement we had!" Vinnie said, turning red, seeing his chances of running his own family going down the drain.

"You're right, because me and you didn't have an agreement. You and Taz did. And furthermore, you must've forgot that I was there when the deal was made and if I recall, the deal was only until Hector was dealt with. Newsflash: Hector is dead!" Kiki turned and walked back into the room.

"I'm not done talking to you!"

"But I'm done talking to you," Kiki said without turning around.

"You disrespectful black bitch!" Vinnie spat, causing Kiki to step back into the hallway and her security to close in.

She waved them off. "I know if Taz was here, you wouldn't have let that come out your mouth," she said and then she slid up on him. She put her mouth to his ear and said, "If you ever call me a bitch again, I'm going to cut your tongue out and wipe my ass with it."

Vinnie wanted to say something, but with the looks Kiki's security team was giving him, he thought better of it.

"I'll be in touch," he said and walked off.

Kiki waved him off and walked back into Meosha's room. She knew he was hot, but he wasn't a threat to her or her empire.

# Chapter 2

"Do you know that that grease ball Vinnie had the nerve to come to the hospital and question me about why I haven't been buying any work from him? Girl, I almost lost it. Then he called me a black bitch!" Kiki told Bella.

They were sitting in Kiki's sunroom with Ares crawling around their feet.

"Why he not on the evening news?" Bella questioned, because she knew how Kiki was.

"Fuck Vinnie! Me cutting him off is enough. Hurting his pockets is enough for me. Besides, I don't know how much favor he has in the Mafia and I don't need a war right now."

"You're right. Nobody really makes money in war time."

Since taking over, both Bella and Kiki had wizened up, more so Bella, because her whole life she'd had nothing to do with anything illegal. So with her taking over the Mexican Cartel, she had to learn on the fly. She executed any and everybody who thought of opposing her place atop the Cartel, which showed them her willingness to be ruthless, but in turn, she awarded houses and cars to all the remaining members' families. She also took notes from Kiki.

Kiki had hit the ground running in regards to running OTF. She'd made major changes to the organization, one of which included putting people in key positions that weren't there before. Kiki had put her cousin Teyona in charge of Atlanta overall, but Teyona's brother Travis was the one who handled all the day-to-day operations as far as collecting money and dropping off work. He only answered to Teyona. Kiki had put Slick in charge of North Carolina. He wasn't really a part of OTF because he had his own crew, but he rocked with them nonetheless. In Miami, there wasn't anybody in charge, but Kiki got Keishana to pick up and drop off for her. In Baltimore, Kiki had a young boy named Niko and in Memphis, she had a dyke named Macy. Kiki had met both of them at All-star weekend in Charlotte a few years ago and they had proved their loyalty on more than one occasion, so Kiki trusted them to hold the fort down.

Kiki's house in ATL had more security than the White House! There were motion sensors all over the ten acre compound with cameras with night vision. Kiki had armed guards that walked around on foot and five Rottweilers that were trained to kill. When Bella was there, she brought her bodyguards, so to try anything would be suicide.

"What do you think Taz would say if he was here right now?" Kiki inquired, crossing her dark chocolate legs.

"Ain't no telling, but I do know he wouldn't allow us to hold the positions we currently have, that's for sure. If it was up to him, we'd be stay at home moms." Bella giggled.

"Who would've thought that two women would be in charge of two of the deadliest crime families in North and South America? Especially your twenty-four-year-young ass."

"You ain't but five years older than me!"

"I'll be thirty next year! Anyway though, I have something to tell you, but you have to promise me that you won't make any rash decisions."

Bella narrowed her eyes and said, "What?"

"Nope! I'm not telling you until you promise you're not going to do anything - at least until you drop that baby," Kiki said, not willing to let Bella do anything to jeopardize Taz's baby.

"I promise. Now what is it?" Bella wanted to know badly.

"Taz had my mama doing some digging before she died and she found out who the big dude was in Haiti. I guess she was planning on telling Taz when he came down here," Kiki said, looking at Bella to judge her reaction.

"Zeus." Bella said the dude's name, shocking Kiki. "I been did my homework. He took over the Zoe Pound Mafia after their last leader got killed," she said, not knowing that Taz and Kiki were the reason he was dead.

"After you drop that baby, we're going to pay him a visit," Kiki said, picking Ares up

"You already know that! Enough of that," Bella said, because thinking about Zeus reminded her of the fact that he and Ares's mother Quanesha had killed her baby boy Junior and that Ares really wasn't her son, even though he would never know. She was raising him as her own, and that's the way it was going to stay.

Quanesha was the mastermind behind the whole kidnapping of Bella and Junior. She'd rocked Taz to sleep and had even had his baby, which was Ares. Taz didn't know that she was Quadree's little sister, the dude he'd gotten locked up for, until she revealed it to him, and by then it was too late. She'd already kidnapped Bella and his son Junior as get-back for him killing her brother. Quanesha had taken Bella's son away from here and in turn, Bella took Ares from her. Too bad she wasn't alive to see it.

"I've been thinking, and as you know, we have the illegal side of things on smash. And I cleaned everything up with the import/export business so the Feds is off that case. You know the wave right now is gambling and betting on sports. What do you think about venturing into that area? It would put us above and beyond," Bella said.

Kiki focused her grey eyes on Bella, thinking about what she'd just told her. Money wasn't really an issue. The investigation firm was bringing in over seven figures a year. And Kiki knew Bella wasn't super strapped because her bitch-ass daddy had been a billionaire. But like the saying went, too much money ain't enough money Kiki knew that it would be all profit, so what did she have to lose?

"What exactly do you have in mind?" Kiki inquired.

"On the west coast they have Las Vegas. On the east coast, there's not too much of anything besides Atlantic City. Miami is already a major tourist spot year round because of the weather. How about we make it THE tourist spot? We can build the most exclusive, state of the art casino in Miami. None of the other casinos here will be able to compete with us. Before long, we will drive the others out of business and we'll be the only one in the city. Can you imagine the amount of money we'd bring in?" Bella started getting excited just thinking about it.

The more Kiki thought it over, the more appeal it had. They couldn't really lose anything, but they could gain a whole lot.

"I'm in. How long do you think it would take?"

"Once we find a location and get the permits, everything will be a go," Bella said confidently.

*That's the easy part*, Kiki thought to herself. The hard part was going to be keeping the Italians out of the way. Kiki remembered what Vinnie was saying about Hector when he was trying to get into the gambling world, but that was Vegas. They were going to be in Miami, a place that was under nobody's control.

***

"Brah, this the life right here," Lo told Slick.

They were in Club Ciroc in Fayetteville enjoying the nightlife. Since putting Slick in charge of North Carolina, he'd really stepped his game up and in turn, Slick put his whole team on. There wasn't a single person on his team that wasn't eating. No man left behind was the motto. They were on top of the world. They had it all: money, hoes, cars, and clothes. They didn't have a care in the world.

Slick had surrounded himself with his main niggas. There was Lo, Twin, Drew, and Quez. They had gone from kicking doors in to running the city. Slick heard Lo's comment about this being *the life* and he agreed, but didn't comment. His mind was occupied with how he could come all the way up and fall back, because Taz's words were ringing in his ear. He'd told him when he first gave him the work not to make a career out of it. Slick just wanted to make sure he'd be able to continue to live like a king when it was all over.

But how much money was enough money? Hustling was so addictive. It was like that bad bitch in every hood with the fire pussy, but the crazy insecure baby daddy. You know the shit is probably going to end badly for somebody, but you still continue to hit that pussy.

A commotion in the middle of the club grabbed his attention, causing him to raise his 5'9" 190 pound frame off of the couch he was sitting on in the VIP section. He walked to the edge of the VIP section and looked down over the crowd and just as he expected, his man Drew was at the center of the commotion. Drew was always in the middle of some shit and he couldn't fight his way out of a wet paper bag, but he'd shoot you to death.

Slick made his way down the steps and into the crowd. When Slick got to the middle, Twin, Quez, and Lo were holding Drew down, but he couldn't see from what. He started laughing when he saw who it was Drew was trying to fight: some broads. Kentavia, Latavia, and Shontavia were sisters, and they were all the way with the shit! Especially the oldest,

Kentavia. She played with guns and all, plus all of them could fight like niggas.

"Nigga, bring your ass on!" Slick said, trying to get him to chill. He turned to walk back up the steps to VIP.

Slick was sitting back down on the couch when they filed back up the steps. Slick could never understand how Drew, being the smallest one at 5'8" and 150 pounds, was always in the most shit. He could understand if it was Lo, who was 6'5" two hundred-something pounds, or Quez, who was 6'3" and about 240, or even Twin, because he was 6'4" and two hundred pounds. But not Drew.

"That bitch tried me!" Drew said in his usual animated way, his shoulder-length dreads swinging.

"You better be glad Latavia ain't cut your stupid ass," Twin said, rubbing his hand across the waves in his head.

"Shut your light bright ass up!" Drew snapped.

Twin was the only light-skinned one of the five. Everybody else was either brown-skinned or dark-skinned.

"How did she try you?" Slick was curious to know.

"She didn't. He grabbed Shantavia's ass and she snapped out," Quez told the truth of the matter.

"Ha, ha!" Lo laughed, showing a glimpse of the permanent slugs he'd paid thirty bands for.

"Fuck them hoes! I got something more exclusive on my radar." Drew rubbed his hands together.

"Who?" Twin asked.

Slick looked his way because he knew Drew was going to say something crazy.

"Kiki's sexy chocolate ass! Hell, I'd even take her twin. It wouldn't make a fuck, but I want the boss," he said, not seeing the look on Slick's face.

"Drew, leave that alone. First off, that's Taz's BM, and second, she'd feel disrespected if you try her knowing you knew Taz."

"Find your ass on the back of them playing cards they give out in the county jail with the missing people on it," Twin joked.

"Nigga, please! I'd tame that pussy, then I'd be the one running OTF. Y'all bullshitting." Drew continued his theatrics, humping the air as if he was in some pussy.

Slick shook his head and sat back on the couch, taking a sip of his drink while they went back and forth. Slick went back to thinking how he could step up his game a little bit, then the idea came to him. He just had to run it by Kiki.

"Shit, nigga, I want Isabella," Twin said.

"Don't let nobody else hear y'all saying this dumb-ass shit, because Bella and Kiki gon' flip," Slick said before heading home to set his plan in motion.

Nicholas Lock

# Chapter 3

"And to what do I owe this pleasure?" Kiki said as Niko stepped into her office at the investigation firm.

"What, I can't come holler at the big homie?" he asked as she came around the desk and gave him a half-hug.

"I don't get no hug?" Alex, Niko's right-hand man, asked.

"Nah, you can get some dap though." Kiki dapped him up.

The last time Kiki had given the nigga a hug he'd grabbed her ass, which almost caused him to lose his life, but Niko had pleaded for her to let it slide. Then she took into account how young he was, so she gave him a pass - his first and last one.

Both Niko and Alex were nineteen years old, but they looked like they were five years younger. Neither one had hair on their faces and were both 6' tall, but that's where their similarities ended. Niko was light-skinned with an athletic build and had long hair that he always kept braided in some type of fashion. His mother was a full-blooded Cherokee Indian. He was also the more laid back of the two. Alex, on the other hand, was the spark plug. He was dark-skinned and stocky. He rocked his hair in a Mohawk that always had three spikes. On account of his mother being Chinese, his eyes were real chinky. Looking at them, you'd think they were pretty boys, but to treat them as such would be a fatal mistake. Their nicknames in Baltimore were Thunder and Lightning. Alex was Thunder because when he struck, it was always loud and violent. Niko was Lightning on account of you'd be dead before you know what hit you. Niko and Alex had run through Baltimore causing mayhem all through the city. Everyone in the city knew and feared their murder game. They were wild cards. You never knew what to expect when it came to the two. Their main hustle had been robbing and extortion, which was what they had been doing when they met Kiki.

Alex and Niko were in Charlotte, North Carolina, the city hosting the NBA's All-star weekend. They'd been patrolling uptown, looking for a victim, when they spotted him. He was walking by himself with a ton of jewels on. They could tell he wasn't one of the dudes that came to All-star week stunting with their re-up money and their best outfits. He solidified it by getting into a black Ferrari 458 Spider with plates that read PAID 4.

"This the one right here," Niko said as they pulled behind him.

What they didn't realize was that while they were locked in watching him, there was somebody watching them. Their victim pulled up on the side of a gas station and disappeared inside. Alex and Niko parked beside him and Niko got out and started smoking a Black and Mild while waiting on their victim to come back out. In the process, an all-white Ferrari pulled up on the other side of the Ferrari Spider and a tall nigga with white-tipped dreads got out. When they saw the thick-ass chain and the life-sized, iced out Tasmanian devil charm, they decided they were going to get him too.

"What's good?" Alex said to the dude, but he just looked at him and kept it pushing, which sent Alex into a rage. "He most definitely getting got!" he stated when the dude walked into the store.

"Let's get this nigga right here first, then we'll get him and kill two birds with one stone. And we can take them whips back to B-More and get a nice chunk of change," Niko said, calculating the numbers in his head of what the chop shop was going to give them for two new Ferraris.

Their first victim bent the corner on the phone and Alex quickly went into action. He grabbed him by the front of the shirt and pushed him on the hood of their red Challenger.

"You know what time it is. Run that!" Alex said, relieving him of his jewels.

"Something funny?" Niko asked, seeing the dude smiling.

"Yeah, you two young niggas is funny. I peeped y'all when I was uptown." He laughed.

"Well, you still getting got!" Alex said

"That's really not a smart move," this dude with the Tasmanian devil charm said, leaning on the edge of the building, lighting up a blunt.

"Not minding your business ain't smart," Niko said, moving in his direction with his gun on him.

"You sure about this?" dude asked, still smoking his blunt.

"Hell yeah."

Niko grabbed the chain and was about to snatch it when a female said, "Pump your brakes."

Niko turned to see a stacked chocolate chick with a cannon to the back of Alex's head. Then he felt the unmistakable feel of a gun pressed against his temple.

"Told you the shit wasn't smart," dude said, grabbing Niko's gun.

"Travis, what I tell you about going off by your lonesome?" Kiki scolded her little cousin. "Now get out of here." She relieved Alex of his pistol "What you want to do with them, Taz?"

"Where y'all niggas from?" Taz asked.

"Baltimore!" Alex said, mean-mugging Kiki, thinking how he was going to try her when he got the chance.

"Go ahead, and they gon' put your face on a T-shirt back home." Kiki saw the look in his eyes.

"How old are y'all?" Taz continued to question them.

"We both sixteen," Niko spoke up.

"Here." Taz gave him his pistol back.

"What you doing?" Kiki looked at him like he was crazy.

"You can't really be mad at these young niggas for trying to eat. That was us back in the day," Taz gave her his reason. "Y'all probably would've came off on this lick, but I know a way y'all can come off every day," Taz told them, seeing their potential.

From that day forward, they got work from Kiki. It was Taz's last day dealing with them. He left it to Kiki. They went from jackboys to dopeboys. They had kept everything on the up and up, which was why Kiki had put them in charge of B-More. Well, Niko was really in charge, but Alex was his right hand, so it was all the same

"Now what are y'all niggas really doing down here?" Kiki asked.

"You know Niko had to come check on his little bitty," Alex said, blowing Niko's spot up.

"Why you doing Ciara like that?" Kiki asked.

Ciara was Niko's pregnant girlfriend. Kiki had met her and taken a liking to her. She was a pretty redbone chick with thick thighs, C-cup breasts, pouty lips, and shoulder-length hair that she always kept done. What Kiki liked was that she wasn't a hood chick. She was from the hood, but she'd gone to school and became a dental hygienist and she was thinking about going back to school to be a dentist. She worshipped the ground Niko walked on.

"I ain't doing her like nothing. She good."

"Okay, nigga. That's a good girl you got. They don't come around too often. You gon' miss her when she's gone." Kiki gave him some knowledge.

"How did this become about my personal life?"

"You're right. So how is everything on your end?" she asked.

"We good! When these new niggas come through, we have to run them down, but other than that, we straight," Alex said.

"Oh, my bad," Meosha said after busting into Kiki's office and seeing that she had visitors.

"You good," Kiki told her and Meosha brought her some paperwork she had to sign.

The whole time, Meosha could feel Alex's eyes on her. When she looked his way, he blew her a kiss, causing her to blush. She didn't know what it was, but she liked the young nigga's style and his not giving a fuck attitude. Last time they were around, he'd tried to holler and she'd shot him down, but it obviously hadn't deterred him.

"Damn, nigga, give my twin her face back," Kiki said, causing Meosha to laugh.

Alex waved her off, continuing to stare at Meosha. When Meosha left the office, he walked out behind her and grabbed her hand, spinning her around to face him.

"Let me go, little boy." She took her hand out of his.

"When you gon' let me take you out?" Alex shot his shot again.

"Why should I?" Meosha raised one of her brows.

"For starters, I want to show you a good time since it's obvious you need it, plus I want to get to know you."

Meosha thought it over and didn't see how it could hurt anything. She'd just have some fun with him and send him on his way.

"Let me see your phone," she told him and then she put her number in it.

"When should I call?" he asked.

"You'll figure it out," she said and then disappeared around the corner.

Alex and Niko wrapped their business up with Kiki and left.

Kiki called Meosha to her office and asked her, "What's up with you and Alex?

"Not a thing. He just wants to take me out," she said, taking a seat.

"How many young boys you know just want to take someone out and not get no pussy? Now you grown, so you make your own decisions, but be careful and don't be mixing business and pleasure."

"I got this," Meosha said and then walked out.

# Chapter 4

Bella had Eve on July 2, 2020. As with all of Taz's kids, she looked just like him. Kiki was there showing her support physically, but her mind was elsewhere. Kiki knew that now that Bella was no longer pregnant, there was going to be nothing holding her back from going at Zeus. Then Vinnie kept calling her phone, making idle threats about what would happen if she didn't start buying work from him again. It looked as if 2020 was gearing up to be a bloody summer. Because she'd had just about enough of Vinnie and his threats, he was going to find himself on the bottom of the Hudson River. And much to her chagrin, Meosha and Alex were in a full-blown relationship. She acted like it wasn't anything serious, but Kiki could tell Meosha had fallen for Alex and vice versa. Maybe Kiki was just jealous because she didn't have anybody special in her life besides her babies, but she was okay with that. There wasn't ever going to be anybody that was going to compare to Taz in her eyes, so she wasn't even looking.

"Penny for your thoughts," Bella said.

"Have you thought about moving on?"

"Moving on from what to what?"

"Another dude." Kiki looked Bella in the eyes.

"No! Taz ruined me for every other dude. My heart still beats for Taz. No one will ever be able to compare. And if I was to move on, I would always be comparing the two and that wouldn't be fair to the other dude, so I'm just going to stay single," Bella confessed.

"Bitch, I feel the same way, and I just bought a vibrating dildo that I call Taz."

"You late to the party! I got two! And one of them has two ends," Bella said and they both busted out laughing.

"On a serious note, I might have to do something to Vinnie. He keeps calling my phone talking reckless" Kiki informed her.

"Vinnie don't really want no smoke! You already know why he's mad. Until he presents himself as a legitimate threat, we're not worrying about him. We got bigger fish to fry. We already got the location downtown for the casino. We're just waiting for all the paperwork to go through with city hall, the zoning commission, and the gambling board in Las Vegas has to give us our gambling license or we'll have a casino that people can't gamble in. And that's like a nigga with a big dick but don't know how to use it: a waste of time! And HKS architects is the company that's going to build it. They're the same company who built the Minnesota Vikings stadium. They told me it's going to be like nothing ever seen before," Bella bragged.

Kiki heard her, but she was more focused on how she was going to deal with Vinnie. He was already too comfortable with his threats. It was only a matter of time before he thought shit was sweet and tried her, which would ultimately lead to his death. She planned on sending him a message that would hopefully deter him from his threats of making a dumb decision that would cost him dearly. She thought of what Taz would do. He'd kill Vinnie and not think twice! Kiki didn't know what it was, but since having her twins, her tolerance level had gone up. Before them, she'd had zero tolerance for anything and anybody.

"Can you at least wait until I heal up?" Bella asked.

"For what?"

"Until you do something to Vinnie. I know you, and I know you over there plotting." Bella read her like a book.

"I'm not gon' do nothing yet. I'm just going to send him a message to let him know he's not untouchable."

\*\*\*

Two weeks later

It was a cloudy overcast day in New York. It had been raining on and off for the last two days and Vinnie welcomed it. He was tired of the sweltering heat. He was leaving his restaurant for the day and couldn't wait to get to his condo uptown. He'd called his favorite escort service, Exotic Escorts, and told them to send a girl to his condo. They already knew that he liked young black women, thick black women, and the darker the better.

Vincent "Vinnie Two Times" Giaconne had worked his way up from a Mafia wannabe to a Capo. It took him twenty-five years, but he'd done it, and now he was in the discussion to become the head of one of the five families. As of now, he was just a Capo in the Genovese family. For him to solidify his spot as a family head, he needed to continue to bring in the bundles of cash he was bringing in by selling to Kiki. Without her cash flow, Vinnie could kiss that top spot goodbye, which was why he was so determined to keep Kiki's business. He was going to get her to cop from him by choice or by force. He really didn't care which one it was just as long as the money came in. Vinnie looked at Kiki and saw a woman that he assumed had landed the spot of running OTF by being Kiana's daughter, but he was going to learn the hard way that Kiki had earned her stripes.

Vinnie climbed into the back of his stretch Navigator and almost jumped out of his skin. There was a light-skinned kid with two braids sitting on the other side of him. Vinnie regained his composure immediately after taking in the kid and thinking he'd just overpower him if need be. He wondered how "Little John", his chauffeur/bodyguard, had allowed him to even get into his car.

"You're in the wrong car, kid," Vinnie said, positioning himself so that he'd be able to launch himself onto the kid if need be.

"Nah, you're just the man I need to see," Niko said, sliding to the other side of the limo, reading Vinnie's mind.

"Little John! Little John!" Vinnie yelled.

The partition rolled down and Vinnie's heart dropped. There was another young boy in the passenger seat, only this one was dark-skinned with a spiked Mohawk. Then Vinnie saw that Little John had a hole in his head the size of a baby's fist.

"Are you crazy? Do you know whose fucking son that was!" Vinnie yelled in full panic mode.

Little John was John "Big John" Gigante's only son. Big John was the current head of the Genovese family. Heads were going to roll behind his murder, and Vinnie's was probably going to be first.

"We honestly don't give a fuck whose son it was. What we do know is this was only a warning. The next time you decide to threaten Kiki, it's gon' be your head with the crater in it," Alex said, pointing the gun at Vinnie.

Vinnie threw his hands up and nodded his head.

With that, Alex and Niko got out and disappeared down an alley, leaving Vinnie to try and figure out how he was going to explain to Big John that his only son was dead and that he was the reason.

# Chapter 5

"Say what? I know for a fact I told y'all not to kill nobody and to just show him shit wasn't sweet! Let me guess: Alex did it, right?" Kiki asked Niko.

He just shrugged his shoulders.

They had Facetimed her to let her know how everything went with Vinnie. Kiki had sent them to holler at Vinnie, maybe rough him up a little bit, but she had stressed to them not to kill anybody.

"I'm glad it's funny, Alex," Kiki said, seeing him smirking "We gon' see how funny it is when I tell Meosha." Kiki hung up, took a deep breath, and leaned her head back against the chair.

"You know them boys retarded," Macy said causing Kiki to snap her head up. She had forgotten she was in a meeting with Macy.

Niko and Alex always found a way to get her frustrated, especially Alex. Macy had come to Atlanta to give Kiki an update on what was going on in Memphis. Kiki looked across her desk at Macy, taking her in. From the outside looking in, you'd never be able to tell that she was a full-blown dyke or the fact that she moved more work than the average nigga. She was 5'7" with milk chocolate-colored skin. She wasn't thick, but she wasn't skinny either. She was what you'd call slim thick. Macy was a girly girl. She acted nothing like a lesbian unless she was trying to holler at a chick. Macy was pretty with or without being dolled up. She could just wake up and go straight to a photo shoot. Macy had features that other women went to plastic surgeons for. Her eyes were perfectly proportioned with naturally long eyelashes and high cheekbones. Her lips which were always coated in MAC lip gloss would put Kylie Jenner's to shame. Everywhere she went, she would get approached by dudes and females trying to holler. Macy was only twenty-five, but she'd been on her own and in the streets since she was fifteen. Macy was from the southside of Memphis, the same side as Yo Gotti. Her mom had kicked her out and she never looked back. Macy took to hustling like a fish to water. Before she knew it, she was making ten bands a day, and that was with mediocre work. But then she met Kiki, and things hadn't been the same since.

\*\*\*

Macy was in Leather and Lace, a strip club in Charlotte throwing money like it was going out of style. With it being All-star weekend, all the top notch strippers had come to the city and were giving it up.

Macy was in one of the VIP sections cutting up. All eyes were on her as she stood by a stage and rained down money on two strippers that were in their birthday suits rubbing each other's pussies. She was wearing a purple bodysuit by Ms. Cat that enhanced the curves she had and some six inch red bottoms. People didn't know whether to watch Macy or the show on stage.

Macy was distracted from the show on stage when a flawless dark-skinned chick flashed by her. When Macy turned, all she saw was ass.

"Say ma," Macy said as she caught up to the dark-skinned girl

"'Sup," she said, facing Macy

*Damn, this bitch bad,* Macy thought to herself before saying, "My face between your legs."

"What's good?" a tall dude with long white-tipped dreads asked the dark-skinned chick as he walked up and slapped her on the ass.

"Her face between my legs. At least that's what she said," the chick said, pointing at Macy

"Word up?" the tall dude asked, smirking.

"My bad, I ain't know she was your girl," Macy said, turning to walk away.

"She not," he said before inviting Macy back to their section in VIP.

It was there Macy learned their names were Kiki and Taz and that they were something like brother and sister. Macy tried to keep up with them as they threw money, but it became clear early on that she was out of her league. Taz was letting the money fly as if he had printed it himself.

When everything calmed down, Taz pulled up on Macy and found out she was a hustler. It was then that he gave her a proposition she couldn't refuse. He was going to supply her with some grade-A coke at a price she didn't think was possible. The whole time they were talking, Macy was checking him out on the low. Macy was gay, but she still recognized a handsome man when she saw one, and she could tell he liked what he saw because as hard as he tried, he couldn't keep his eyes from wandering over her body. In the end, Macy left All-star weekend with the plug she'd been looking for. Once she flooded Memphis with the high-end coke, she took the city by storm. Then when Kiki took over OTF and gave her a spot, she was untouchable. She went from supplying Memphis to all of Tennessee.

"So what's the deal, Macy?" Kiki looked across her desk at Macy and hoped she wasn't bringing more bad news because Kiki wasn't sure she could handle another situation at the moment.

"Everything my way is good. I got that situation handled with them young boys in Knoxville too."

Macy was a hustler through and through, so when it came to that rah-rah shit, she wasn't with it. If it didn't make dollars, it didn't make sense was the motto she lived by. She wasn't necessarily with all the gunplay, but since she'd linked up with OTF, whenever she had a real issue, Kiki would send someone to handle it. That way, Macy could focus on running it up.

"I'm glad to hear that, because I definitely wasn't trying to hear no more unsavory news."

"What them boys got going on now?" Macy asked, referring to Niko and Alex.

As Kiki got to telling Macy what had happened, Teyona walked into the office.

"Hey Teyona," Macy said, looking her up and down, licking her lips. Macy wanted Teyona just as bad as a nigga in prison wanted freedom. Every time they were around each other, Macy would make slick remarks, but Teyona would never bite. Kiki had told Macy that Teyona didn't rock like that, but Macy had turned out plenty of straight females.

As with all of Kiki's family, Teyona was dark-skinned with full lips and thick hips. She had perky B-cups, no stomach, and a nice round booty. Today she had on a pair of tan Chanel pants that made her butt sit up higher, a white Chanel blouse, and white open toe Chanel pumps that showed off her pedicure.

"What it do, Macy?" Teyona responded.

"I'm trying to figure it out," Macy said, uncrossing and crossing her legs, making the skirt she wore rise up.

"Girl, boo." She waved her off. "Kiki, Slick is here and he trying to holler at you ASAP."

"Go ahead and bring him back," she said. "Leave my cousin alone, Macy," Kiki said once Teyona had left to go get Slick.

"I ain't doing nothing, Kiki." Macy grinned, showing off her perfectly-aligned teeth.

"Tell me anything. How long you gon be in the A?"

"A few days. You know I'm a strip club junky."

"Ok, we gon' get up before you bounce," Kiki said as Slick walked into her office.

"Damn, Macy! Where your pretty ass been hiding at?" Slick said, strolling into the room.

"Here and there. You know I be low-key."

"I'm gon' be in Memphis soon and I'm expecting you to show me around too."

"Just give me a ring," Macy said, holding up her iPhone as she walked out of Kiki's office.

"What's the business?" Slick asked.

"Same old thing, just trying to get that bag."

"Me too, which just so happens to be the reason I popped up on you."

"I'm listening." Kiki kicked her Gucci heels off and curled her feet under her.

"Peep game. I got North Carolina locked up, but I'm trying to venture out and put my thing down in another state. I'm trying to really stack my chips so I can fall back like Taz did," Slick said. He slid Taz's name in there to try and get some points because he knew now she felt when it came to Taz.

Kiki looked him over, thinking to herself. The whole time Slick was shooting his pitch, Kiki had her brow raised. He didn't have his state under control like he thought.

"I don't think you're ready to hold down two states, especially since you don't have North Carolina on lock like you think. I just got word a couple days ago that you lost control of a portion of Fayetteville to a crew called GMC," Kiki said, letting him know she was on her shit.

"Nah, they're not even a factor. We allow them to do the little bit that they do."

"Oh yeah?" She cocked her head to the side. "Check this out." Kiki handed him her Galaxy S20.

Slick took the phone and it was showing a video that some GMC dudes had posted on Facebook and Instagram showing them jumping his man Drew. Slick could only shake his head. He was slipping because he knew nothing about it. He was going to chew his crew out for making him look bad in front of Kiki.

"That's minor. It'll be handled accordingly."

"I have no doubt about it, but it shows me that everything isn't in order your way. Don't get me wrong; I expect opposition to arise. But for them to post it on the internet shows me that they neither fear nor respect you. So in a couple months, I'll give it some thought." She stood up, signaling to him that their meeting had concluded.

"Bet, bet," Slick said standing up. He wasn't feeling her answer, but he respected it. He was about to make life miserable for them GMC niggas and anybody who fucked with them.

# Chapter 6

"You have my word, Big John. I'm going to make them pay," Vinnie said.

"I know you are, Vinnie, because if you don't, you're going to have to answer for me burying my son," Big John said.

They were on the phone and Vinnie had just told him he knew who was responsible for killing Little John. Vinnie neglected to mention that it was Kiki because he still felt like there was a chance he'd get her to fall in line. Vinnie still had his mind on being a don. A few days ago a thought occurred to him. Why should he keep trying to get Kiki back on his side when he could just replace her? He thought he had just the right person, which was why he was in Fayetteville, North Carolina. He'd met Slick one time while he was in Atlanta and Vinnie could see that Slick had a lot of potential. Vinnie knew Slick had the type of personality where he would always crave more, so he was going to give Slick an offer he couldn't refuse.

Vinnie and his two bodyguards pulled up outside of Fat Daddy's and waited for Slick to show up. Vinnie was prepared to wait all day. He didn't have to wait long. Slick pulled up and got out of a blue Mustang with the black racing stripe. Vinnie's bodyguards pulled up on Slick and said, "Our boss wants to talk to you."

At first Slick was going to go for his gun, thinking it was some kind of trickery by the GMC crew, but he knew they would've just started shooting, so he made his way over to the black Yukon.

"Vinnie!" Slick said, climbing in the back and seeing who the two beefy bodyguards were calling their boss.

"Slick, my man." Vinnie extended his hand "Long time no see."

"What brings you to my city?" Slick questioned.

"I needed to holler at you. How's life been treating you?"

"I'm good. I could be better, but that's life, ya know?" he admitted.

"Well, I think I can make your life a whole lot better."

"I'm listening." Slick's curiosity was aroused.

"I'll get right to it. I have an endless supply of coke or whatever other kind of drug you want."

"Why are you telling me this?" Slick balled his face up, thinking Kiki had sent Vinnie to test him.

"Whoa, whoa, whoa, it's nothing like that," Vinnie said hurriedly, seeing Slick get upset. "If you didn't notice, me and Kiki no longer do business together."

Slick didn't know this, but the more he thought about it, the more it made sense because Kiki got work from Bella. This could be his chance to expand his domain. Kiki couldn't get mad because technically he wasn't OTF.

"Okay, I'm with it, but what are the prices?"

"If you buy at least thirty bricks, I'll give them to you for ten a pop." Vinnie sweetened the deal by saying, "And on top of that, I'll give you the pounds of weed for a thousand apiece, but you have to get a minimum of two hundred."

"What kind of weed is it?"

Vinnie reached under his seat and pulled out a Ziploc bag filled to the top with weed. Slick grabbed the bag and opened it. Instantly, the truck filled up with a pungent smell. Slick grabbed a bud out of the bag and knew off the rip that it was White Widow. He calculated the numbers in his head and knew it was going to cost him half a million dollars to do the deal, and that was all the money he had put up to the side. But he knew he'd be able to triple his money with the quality of weed and coke Vinnie had.

"Alright, it's a deal."

"There's one more stipulation that I forgot to mention," Vinnie said and his bodyguards cocked their weapons back and turned in their seats to face Slick and Vinnie.

"What?" Slick asked, ignoring the guns.

"You have to kill Kiki."

\*\*\*

"It's bullshit!" Bella vented to Kiki.

"You should've known it wasn't going to be that easy. You know the Mafia controls the gambling board. Did you think they were just going to roll over and let you eat a slice of their pie without greasing no palms or nothing?" Kiki asked, bouncing D'Angel on her knee

"I wouldn't grease their palms if my life depended on it! It's okay though because two can play that game. They're about to learn that I'm nothing to play with!" Bella worked herself up. "You still got an issue with Vinnie?"

"He ain't called threatening me no more. So I would think not."

"I'm gon' do this shit the way Taz would! If I can't make no money, then nobody's making money!" Bella yelled, causing Eve to start crying.

Kiki just shook her head as Bella breastfed Eve. Kiki had to prepare herself mentally for the war that was more than likely going to happen. Kiki knew Bella wasn't going to go for getting muscled out of starting a casino, and that meant she was about to start a war with the Mob.

With OTF and the Mexican Cartel teamed up, Kiki didn't believe they'd lose, but she knew they were going to take some losses. She just wasn't aware of the amount. Kiki was surprised Bella hadn't mentioned the Zoe Pound leader Zeus.

As if reading her mind, Bella said, "We're about to pay Zeus a visit first,"

Kiki could only smile because this was the type of shit she was built for. The only person that rivaled her in the battlefield was Taz, and he was dead and gone.

"Let's do this," Kiki said.

***

Three days later

Kiki had recruited her young boys Niko and Alex to accompany her, Bella, and ten members of the Mexican Cartel as they went to Haiti to deal with Zeus. They were on Bella's private jet en route to Haiti when Belk said, "Remember to save Zeus for me." Everybody except Alex nodded their head in agreement.

"I can't make no promises. When the bullets start to fly, I go for what I know. I'm not gon' be trying to pick and choose my targets. Besides, this the nigga that killed the big homie Taz's firstborn. Why shouldn't I make him proud by deading the nigga?"

Kiki was going to check him, but Bella beat him to it. Bella stood up in her army fatigues and walked over to where Alex sat

"Alex, right?" Bella asked, squatting down in front of him putting her hands on his thighs.

"Yeah." He smiled, eyeing the print between her legs

"It's obvious you don't know who I am." Bella rubbed his thighs.

"Of course I do. You're the chick that runs the Mexican Cartel," he said as his dick swelled up from Bella's touch.

"Ha, you're right, but I'm also Taz's baby mother," Bella stated, grabbing his dick and balls in a vice-like grip

"Aahh!" Alex yelled, trying to go for his gun.

But Bella pulled hers and pointed it at his dick, "If you would've done your research, you'd have known that. Zeus killed my son Junior, so if you deny me the pleasure of getting my revenge, no one, including God, is going to be able to save you," she said, looking him in the eyes. He nodded. "Good!" Bella got up and went back to her seat

"Fuck you smirking at, nigga?" Alex asked Niko.

"Y'all get it together!" Kiki said. "We almost there."

Everyone chilled as Kiki and Bella gave them the plan on how the assault was going down. As they broke the game plan down, Kiki took in the ten Cartel dudes Bella had brought. They ranged from short to tall, athletic to heavyset, but one thing they all had in common was the look in their eyes. Kiki knew blood lust when she saw it and she saw it in all their eyes.

There was one in particular that caught her eye. He was maybe 5'10" and stocky. He had tattoos all over his face, one of which was a big-ass dragon that covered the whole right side of his face. The tail wrapped around the back of his head and into his mouth.

"That's Dragon," Bella whispered. "You see all those yellow stars on the side of his head? That's his body count, and he just turned twenty-three."

Kiki counted forty-nine stars. He had more bodies than her and he was six years younger than she was. She was impressed, but she was going to see how he maneuvered in battle then Kiki would say if he got her approval.

Nicholas Lock

# Chapter 7

They wasted no time. Once the plane touched down in Port-au-Prince, they went on their search. They had four Dodge Ram 1500's waiting at the airport. The ten Cartel members got in three and Bella, Kiki, Alex, and Niko got in the other one. They were ready for war! Everyone donned bulletproof vests and carried some kind of machine gun.

"Where exactly am I going?" Kiki asked, driving.

"All I remember is driving down this road and pulling up to a white house," Bella said from the passenger seat.

Kiki shook her head and called Meosha. "Go in my office and tell me that address that's on my desk. It's on a big brown envelope."

Kiki keyed the address into her GPS and swerved off. They rode for about thirty minutes and came upon a roadblock. Only it wasn't the police; it was a group of dread heads in camouflage fatigues welding choppas.

"Da roads closed," one said to Kiki when she rolled her window down.

"It looks fine to me," Kiki said.

"What mi say! Road closed, turn around!" he yelled, causing the others in the group to start making their way towards the truck.

Thinking Bella was in danger, the trucks behind them opened fire on the group, cutting them down.

"So much for that." Kiki gunned the engine.

They bent the corner and saw about a hundred people blocking the street. Alex was about to let off into the crowd, but Niko stopped him.

"It's some kind of parade," Niko said, noticing that most of the people dancing around.

"What are we going to do now?" Alex asked.

"I'm getting out," Bella said and everyone followed suit.

There were people everywhere. They were having some kind of festival because there were people in masks and costumes. They also noted that there were dudes walking around with AK's and AR15's. Everyone grabbed their guns and fanned out into the crowd. Bella showed Zeus's picture to her soldiers and told them to be on the lookout. They hadn't been walking for five minutes when Kiki saw him. Zeus was standing off to the side as another dread head spoke to him in an animated fashion and started pointing in the direction of where they had parked the trucks.

"I think we need to go, and I mean right now!" Niko said, seeing the same thing Kiki was.

Everyone started making their way to the trucks when a dude grabbed Bella and started to dry hump her. On his second hump, his head exploded. One of the esses blew his brains all over the street. Kiki expected there to be pandemonium, but people kept doing what they were doing as if they were used to it. They made it to the trucks just as the shots started

KAH! KAH! KAH! KAH! KAH!

Everybody ducked and turned to see Zeus and a mob of niggas shooting guns their way.

"Yeeeaahh!" Alex said, firing his AK in their direction.

Now there was pandemonium! People were running and ducking, trying to dodge the bullets.

"Don't kill Zeus!" Bella yelled, shooting a customized pink choppa.

TAT! TAT! TAT! TAT! TAT!

"Get to the trucks!" Kiki yelled because they were at a disadvantage.

The Cartel members surrounded Bella as they fired their guns and made their way to the trucks. Zeus was only about thirty feet away, but they were keeping it so hot that no one could get a shot off. They got to the trucks and reversed all the way down the road.

"Fuck!" Bella yelled once they had the trucks going in the right direction. "He was right there! I almost had him!"

"You might get a second chance," Niko said, looking out the back window.

Bella looked in the rearview mirror and saw three old F-150's coming up behind them with a dread head hanging out the sunroof.

"Shit!" Kiki said.

"I'm not dying in Haiti!" Alex yelled, leaning out the window and letting his choppa talk.

When Alex started shooting, the esses followed suit and started shooting at the trucks behind them. They turned off when the dread head that was hanging out the sunroof slumped over.

"Fuck I thought," Niko said, leaning back inside the truck.

"Don't let your guard down, I have a feeling we'll be seeing some more action soon," Kiki said, not knowing how right she was.

They got about two miles down the road, then it was blocked off by a dump truck with Zeus and a mini army standing in the way. Kiki slammed on the brakes as Zeus and his crew started sending hot balls their way. The truck behind them slammed into the back of Kiki's truck, lifting it into the air. When it came down, it landed on the hood of the truck that had hit them. Kiki, Bella, Niko, and Alex jumped out of the immobilized truck and started trading shots with Zeus.

Kah! Kah! Kah!

Tat! Tat! Tat!

It sounded like the Fourth of July. Kiki knew it wouldn't be long before they'd get taken down, so they had to think fast.

But help came from where they least expected it: the police. Haiti's finest pulled up on the other side of the dump truck and started shooting at the Zoe Pound. There was an ongoing conflict between the Zoe Pound and the Haiti police department. The Zoe Pound was stuck in the middle of the two sides with nowhere to go. By the time Zeus realized the position he was in, more than half of his team had been gunned down and were steadily dropping. He started to run, but Bella and Kiki were on his ass like the 9-Trey niggas were on Tekashi 6ix9ine. He ducked behind a house as Kiki put a round in his leg and Bella put one in his back. They ran behind the house and found Zeus crawling on his stomach.

"Yeah, bitch!" Bella kicked him in his side and he flipped over on his back.

Bella shot him in his shoulder, causing him to cry out.

"No, motherfucka! Don't you holler!" Bella stood over him, pointing the AK in his face.

"Please don't kill me!" Zeus begged. "Mi take ya to ya son if ya let mi live."

"Y'all killed my baby!" Bella croaked as her eyes began filling with water.

Bella forced the barrel into his mouth and he mumbled out, "Me swear he's alive."

"He's playing you, Bella. Blow his top off!" Kiki tried coaxing her.

"Take me to him and if you're lying, I'm gon' kill you, bring you back, and kill you again," Bella growled.

By this time, all the shooting had stopped and everyone was standing around Bella.

"Pick him up and put him in the back of the truck," Bella ordered.

As the Cartel members carried him to one of the trucks, the police just looked on. They hated Zeus and the Zoe Pound so much they wanted to see him dead.

Kiki, Bella, Niko, and Alex got in the truck and Dragon and another esse got in the truck bed with Zeus. Zeus had them drive into a deeply-wooded area. After driving for about five miles, the woods cleared out and they drove into what appeared to be the Zoe Pound's headquarters. There were dudes walking around with all types of weaponry, which was focused on the three trucks as they came to a stop in the middle of the camp.

"If this goes bad, you'll be the first to die," Alex said to Zeus through the back window.

They went crazy when they saw Zeus in the truck bed bleeding out. They trained their guns on the trucks and started rapidly speaking a foreign language. Not wanting to be stuck inside the trucks if the Zoe Pound started shooting, everyone got out with their guns up and ready. Seeing the situation quickly deteriorating, Kiki jumped into the truck bed, grabbed Zeus by his hair, and put the AK15 to his head.

"If we die, he dies!" Kiki yelled.

"Oh my God!" Bella screamed and took off running towards a group of kids that had come out of a building to see what the commotion was.

Before any of the Zoe Pound got a chance to grab her, Zeus put his hand up and said something in Creole that stopped them in their tracks.

"It can't be," Kiki said as Bella picked a little boy up with a head full of hair.

"Ya have ya son. Now go!" Zeus yelled before passing out.

Kiki let the Zoe Pound member get Zeus as Bella walked back up with Junior. As soon as they got close, Kiki could tell it was Taz Junior just by looking at him.

The Zoe Pound let them leave without incident. The whole ride back to the plane, all Kiki could think about was that Taz would've killed Zeus, no if's, and's, or but's about it. Kiki knew Zeus wasn't going to let it go that he'd been basically humiliated in front of his people. Kiki was going to have to make sure he was dealt with real soon because like the 48 Laws of Power said, crush your enemies totally.

# Chapter 8

Bella couldn't be happier. She had her son back and everything was going good. Junior was a little standoffish at first, but after a week of TLC, he was a normal two-year-old. Junior and Ares were getting along okay and Eve was getting bigger by the day. The only issue was that every time Bella would dote on Junior, Ares would start to cry. He wasn't used to having to share her affection, especially with another boy. Keishana couldn't get enough of Junior. He looked more like Taz than any of his other kids.

"Be nice, Ares," Bella said, seeing him snatch a toy from Junior. "Whew! Am I glad y'all are here," she said as Kiki and Keishana walked into her house.

Bella had kept the house she and Taz had in Miami then she'd bought the house beside it too and had it added onto hers, making it the largest house on the block. Kiki sat the twins D'Angel and Damiyana on the floor to play with Junior and Ares. Immediately, Damiyana took the toy Ares was playing with and looked at him as if to say "and what?" Everyone busted out laughing.

"I told you she was mean," Keishana said.

"She only nine and a half months and she acting like when she gets older," Bella said.

"I'm gon' be beating her ass too," Kiki commented on Bella's statement.

"Only because Taz not here, because if he was, you know you wouldn't put your hands on her," Bella reminded her.

"I miss that nigga," Keishana said.

"Me too," Bella and Kiki said in unison.

They all stared off into space, each one reliving some of the good moments they'd had with Taz. Kiki was the first one to break the trance.

"Bella, I know you're getting reacquainted with Junior, but keep in mind we got issues that need to be dealt with."

"I'm two steps ahead of you. You must ain't watched the news lately?" Bella said.

Kiki got up and cut the TV on the news so she could see what the hell Bella was talking about.

"This is Ashley Monroe for Channel Five news and I'm coming to you live from Caesar's Palace in Las Vegas, where there have been two mass shootings, one at the MGM Grand and one not an hour ago here at Caesar's Palace. So far police are saying that a group of Hispanic men walked into both casinos and opened fire. The motive is unknown at the time."

Kiki cut the TV off and looked at Bella in a new light. She didn't think Bella had the ruthlessness in her, but obviously Taz had rubbed off on her.

"What about those innocent people?" Keishana asked, picking D'Angel up.

"What about them? This is bigger than them! If I can't eat, then can't nobody eat!"

Kiki understood Bella's game now. She was going to make it where the casinos started to lose money because they were going to have to temporarily shut down while the police sorted everything out.

"And what's the plan when they open back up?" Kiki wondered.

"I'm gon' send some more shooters. Sooner or later these Mafia pussies will get the message. Then we'll see if they want to talk. You know those casinos are billion dollar machines. If they're shut down for more than a week, I guarantee you they'll come calling." Bella ran down her game plan.

"But how are they going to know how to reach out to you though?" Keishana was lost.

"Oh, they know." Bella smirked.

\*\*\*

Meanwhile, in New York…

The heads of the Mafia's Five Families were having an emergency meeting concerning the recent events in Las Vegas. There was Anthony Franzese of the Colomba family; Alphonso "Alphie" Trinchers of the Gambino family; Joseph "JoJo" Acetturo of the Lucchese family; Timothy "Tom-Tom" Masselli of the Bonanno/Massino, family who was also the don that was out of favor with the other family dons. He was the one the Feds were investigating. Then at the head of the table was the Mafia's governing body and the head of the Genovese family, John "Big John" Gigante.

"Who the hell does she think she is?" Alphie asked, being the hot headed one.

"You were the one that was so opposed to her opening the casino in Miami when all we had to do was allow her to open it, then demand a cut," Anthony Franzese said.

"We're losing boatloads of money with the casinos closed," JoJo said.

"And her message said she's going to ensure that the casinos stay closed until the gambling board approves her to open the casino," Tom-Tom stated.

"So what do you guys think we should do about it?" Big John asked. "Because honestly, I have some pressing matters that need my undivided attention, particularly avenging my son's death."

"You have my deepest condolences," Anthony Franzese said

"I say we kill her!" Alphie pounded the table.

"So you want us to go to war with the Mexican Cartel and risk our lives? Because if you didn't know, they're a formidable force. We could just allow her to open the damn casino," JoJo spoke up.

"I think we're looking at this the wrong way. Why not let her open it up and see how it goes? If it goes well, it'll pave the way for us to open casinos in Miami as well, which is an untapped market. Then if she fails, we still win. So I think it's a win-win situation," Big John, the thinker of the five, said.

"Let's vote. All in favor of allowing her to open the casino, raise your hand," Tom-Tom said, and everyone raised their hands except Alphie.

"Four to one," Big John said.

"Y'all are going to regret this! Mark my words! Next she'll think she can move into Las Vegas. Then what?" Alphie said  before he walked out.

"He'll be okay. What's the situation with avenging Little John's death?" JoJo asked.

"I have Vinnie on it. He's found out that the two young niggers that did it are from Baltimore and are named Niko and Alex," Big John said. He didn't know that the whole ordeal was orchestrated by OTF's matriarch Kiki, somebody that the five dons didn't know anything about.

"You have faith in him?" Anthony Franzese inquired.

"He better have faith in himself. His head is on the line – literally," Big John stated.

They all chuckled because they knew what that meant. Vinnie was in a real do or die situation.

They left Big John's estate in upstate New York without a care in the world. But there was somebody watching them that was going to turn their world upside down.

# Chapter 9

"Kiki, you have a visitor," her secretary buzzed her.

"Who is it?" She wasn't expecting anyone, plus it was the end of the day and she was ready to get home to her babies and a hot bath.

"An Agent Edwards," she responded.

"Agent Edwards...Agent Edwards. Where do I know that name from?" Kiki asked herself out loud. "Oh shit!" she said when she realized that he was the detective that had arrested Taz for the murder charge and the one that Quadree and Gutha were in cahoots with. But what did he want with her? "Send him in."

"What's the reason a federal agent is stopping by my office asking to see me? This is an investigation firm, but I'm sure you don't need any help in that. At least, I hope not," Kiki said, taking in the agent as he stepped inside her office.

"How about money laundering, racketeering, and the RICO act? Not to mention a host of murders. We know Taz didn't kill Quadree because we never found the murder weapon. The gun he had on him hadn't been fired. And since you were his partner in crime, I know you were there and that you were the one who killed Quadree," he said, taking it upon himself to have a seat.

"I didn't offer you a seat."

"You've done okay for yourself since taking over for your mother," he stated while looking around her office.

Kiki was thirty-eight hot! If she believed she could get away with it, she'd put a bullet between his eyes. But Taz had taught her to never lose her composure because uncontrolled emotions led to big problems, so she was going to bide her time.

"What do you want? I don't have time for your games."

"Nothing; just wanted to stop by and have a chat," he said nonchalantly. He focused his icy blue eyes on Kiki's grey ones.

Kiki matched his stare, all the while sizing him up. He was about 6'2" and slim with short blond hair. She felt like she could take him if need be.

Kiki stood up and smoothed her dark blue Prada skirt down. She walked around her desk and opened her door up

"I take it you want me to leave."

"Unless you have a warrant for my arrest, I suggest you leave." She opened the door wider

Agent Edwards smiled and stood up. "Watch the company you keep," he whispered. He winked and disappeared down the hallway.

***

"This shit is a gold mine!" Drew said. He'd just run through two ounces of powder in thirty minutes.

"Tell me about it," Twin said.

"I don't know how you found this spot, but this shit is bananas," Lo said, making a sale.

They were in a small town in South Carolina called Greenville. Slick had gotten the work from Vinnie and he, Drew, Lo, and Twin had set up shop in South Carolina. Quez had stayed in Fayetteville for two weeks and the thirty birds were almost gone. They were running through the pounds like water. Greenville was right by Clemson, which had Clemson University. All the students loved the high-end coke and exotic weed. The way things were moving, Slick was going to make all his niggas millionaires. He knew he could hold another state down. All Kiki would have had to do was put her trust in him. When Vinnie told him he had to kill Kiki, he'd had no choice but to agree, because if he didn't, Vinnie's bodyguard was going to kill him.

In all actuality, he had no plans on harming one hair on her head. There was no way he could betray Taz like that. Taz gave him a chance when nobody else would. Slick was going to get rich real quick and tell Vinnie to go fuck himself. Biggie was right when he said mo' money mo' problems, because the more money Slick made the more issues that popped up. He'd yet to deal with the GMC issue and they'd just shot one of his spots up.

"What the fuck?" Drew said as the lights went off.

"I thought you paid the light bill," Lo said, flipping the light switch on and off.

"I did, nigga!" Slick said.

"Yo, I can't see shit out here in these backwoods," Twin said, trying to see out the window.

Boom! Boom! Boom!

Klah! Klah! Klah! Klah!

Whoever was shooting was keeping it so hot that they didn't have a chance to return any shots. Whatever they were shooting was knocking the bricks on the house loose, and neither of them wanted to get hit by them bullets.

"Ay, Lo!" Slick called, but didn't get an answer. "Lo!" Slick called again, but still didn't get a response

Everybody started fearing the worst until they heard him yell, "Fuck wrong with y'all!"

KAH! KAH! KAH! KAH! KAH! KAH! KAH!

Lo had crawled out the back door and was on the side of the house shooting a Draco. Lo was shooting and walking towards a grey minivan that the shots were coming from. Drew, Slick, and Twin finally joined in. Lo had the shooters trying to dodge the 223 bullets coming out of the Draco. They were Swiss cheesing the minivan! The driver's side door opened and the driver was pushed out onto the ground. Another dude took his place in the driver's seat and swerved off, leaving the driver face down in the street.

Lo and Slick walked over to him and Lo used his foot to flip him over. Slick instantly recognized him. He was one of the young boys that use to hustle up the street, but when Slick came through with better work and prices, their flow had dried up, which caused their money to dry up. Now they were trying to run Slick off. But it was going to take a lot more than some misplaced bullets to do that.

***

While Slick was having issues in South Carolina, Quez was having issues with the GMC niggas in Fayetteville.

"I want y'all to try me like y'all tried Drew! Jump me!" he yelled.

There was about twenty GMC niggas outside of the Taco Bell on Raeford Road and it was only Quez, Eric, and Nick Beans. Under any other circumstances, the twenty GMC niggas would've been hopped on they ass, but Quez being as big as he was, they weren't in a rush to try their hand.

Then Boom-Boom stepped up. "Nigga, what's up?" Boom-Boom said, taking his shirt off.

Boom-Boom was Taz's little nigga and he was all the way with the shits! If Taz was alive, he'd dead the whole situation because he fucked with both of them, plus he rocked with the head nigga of GMC, AJ.

"Nigga, I'm what's up!" Quez said.

To the naked eye, you'd relate Boom-Boom and Quez to David and Goliath because of the size difference. Quez outweighed Boom-Boom by almost a hundred pounds and at 6'3", he was half a foot taller, but Boom-Boom gave it up! As they squared off, one of the GMC niggas pulled a gun and started shooting in the air, which proved to be a fatal mistake. While he was shooting in the air, putting holes in the clouds, Eric pulled a P90 Ruger out and started putting holes in him.

Everybody scattered, leaving the GMC nigga dead in the parking lot. He was only eighteen. Blood had been spilled, a life had been lost. Now there was no turning back and no peace.

Nicholas Lock

# Chapter 10

"Am I that bitch, or am I that bitch?" Bella yelled, making Kiki look at her like she was crazy.

"Bitch!" Junior yelled, repeating what he heard his mother say.

"No, baby! You can't say that," Bella scolded him, kissing him on his cheek.

"What's wrong with you, girl?" Kiki asked.

"I just got word that the gambling board signed off. We about to be casino owners, and you know even without their okay, I told the builders to keep going. So they should be done by the middle of next year!" Bella said excitedly.

Kiki was just as excited. She just wasn't showing it. She had a lot going on in her life right now. From Agent Edwards paying her a visit to Slick moving into another state even after she'd told him not to. And not only that, he'd killed one of the dudes that OTF was in the process of recruiting. Slick wasn't OTF and he was free to do what he wanted, but Kiki thought they had an understanding.

She'd sent some OTF members back to Haiti to try and knock Zeus off, but it was like he'd fallen off the face of the earth. Kiki hoped he'd died from his wounds, but she knew her luck wasn't that good. To make matters worse, Kiki had been receiving news that somebody fitting Zeus's description had been spotted in Little Haiti and the Pork and Beans projects lately. That was really the reason Kiki had come to Miami: to see if Zeus was just walking around. Meosha had tagged along just to get out of Atlanta.

It was times like this she wished Taz was alive. He'd ease her mind and her body. Whew! Her pussy was starting to drip thinking about the way Taz used to sex her. He was her first and only lover. and most likely her last. Taz had been dead over a year now, but it seemed like just yesterday they'd been together.

"Damn, girl, what's the matter with you?" Bella asked, seeing Kiki wasn't really taking part in her excitement.

"I miss Taz," Kiki confessed.

"We all do, but I know he wouldn't have wanted us to still be mourning him," said Bella.

"I know, but that doesn't change the fact. What do you think he doing right now?"

"He probably done ran down on the devil and took his spot. You know how he is. I started to say he might be up there with God, but you know he was a little too evil to make it into heaven."

"Oh my God! Can you imagine the convo him and God had?" Kiki laughed.

"That's what I want to see: you laughing. You know what? I know what we need. Let's hit the club and let our hair down," Bella suggested.

"I ain't been out in so long."

"Exactly! So tonight we going out: me, you, Meosha, and Keishana. So call them and let them know to be ready."

"I'll let them know. I know Meosha gon' come. Let me get out of here so I can hit the mall and get something to wear."

"Don't make me come looking for you," Bella warned.

"Girl, bye!" Kiki said, walking out.

"Bye!" Junior yelled.

\*\*\*

One thing couldn't nobody say was that Kiki, Meosha, Bella, and Keishana couldn't dress. They were on some rip the runway shit! Niggas and bitches alike couldn't take their eyes off the foursome as they got out of their foreigns. Kiki drove

Taz's cocaine white Ferrari with Meosha in the passenger seat and Bella had just bought the 2020 Rolls Royce Wraith that was royal blue and jubilee silver. She and Keishana were shutting shit down! Kiki had hit the Fendi store in the mall and bought her and Meosha matching minis that had an open slit in the front and the back was open. The only difference was that Kiki's was hot pink while Meosha's was lime green. She also got them Fendi totes that matched their minis. Kiki finished the outfits with six inch stilettos.

Bella and Keishana didn't disappoint in the clothes department either. Bella was wearing a Gucci mini, but hers was black and had the interlocking G's all over it in silver and a pair of black and silver Gucci heels. Keishana, not to be left out, had bought a powder blue Alexander McQueen mini and some white Balenciaga boots that came all the way up her thick thighs. Kiki's, Meosha's, and Keishana's bright miniskirts stood out against their skin tones. Kiki and Meosha had gotten their hair done too. Kiki got hers washed and conditioned then laid down so that it was bone straight. Meosha just brought a lime green wig that matched her mini. Keishana didn't go all out with the hair. She'd just gotten a blowout, but she'd gotten some powder blue lip gloss made by Gucci mane's wife Keyshia Dior. Bella kept it simple and was wearing her hair down.

As they walked up to the door of Club 305, they saw looks of envy on the chicks' faces and looks of lust in the niggas' eyes. Then Meosha only added to their lust because her mini already barely covered her ass, but somehow she had it where the bottom of her ass was out. The slit in the front was originally only about four inches, but Meosha had it altered to where it was wide open, showcasing her flat stomach, and her nipples were playing peek-a-boo.

They entered the club and were led straight to the VIP section that was roped off. There were bottles of Ace of Spades on ice and a big bottle of Peach Ciroc.

"It's lit in here," Meosha said, taking a seat on one of the couches

"That's a fact!" Bella replied, turning a bottle of Ace of Spade up.

"You killing 'em in that dress," Keishana told Meosha.

"Oh, bitch, I know! And I want to borrow them Balenciaga boots," Meosha stated. "This my shit!" she yelled, hopping up as Money Bag Yo and Megan Thee Stallion's hit song came on.

They all hit the dance floor and put in work. Bella and Kiki were dancing with each other and Meosha was throwing her ass on Keishana.

Bella surprised them all with her game. For her to be Mexican, she had a dance game like a sista.

"Oh Twin!" Kiki yelled as Meosha dropped into a split and started popping her ass.

Not to be outdone, Keishana grabbed her ankles and began popping one cheek at a time. Then Bella joined in and put her hands on the floor and started throwing her ass in circles. Kiki walked up behind Bella, grabbed her hips, and began stroking her like she had a dick. Everybody in the club stopped what they were doing to watch the four bad bitches do their thing.

A brown-skinned dude got on the floor behind Meosha and got up on her ass. She looked back at him and started throwing her ass on him. Then a dude in a white Prada outfit got behind Keishana and they started grinding on each other. Seeing this as an invitation, two light-skinned dudes tried to get between Kiki and Bella, but they deaded it with the looks they gave them. They danced for another two songs and then went back to the VIP section, where they proceeded to get pissy drunk.

"Bella, I ain't know you had moves like that," Kiki slurred.

"How do you think I got Taz?" she said, rocking her hips from side to side.

"TMI," Keishana said.

"When was the last time you got some dick, Keishana?" Bella asked, drunk as hell.

They all knew her situation with her being HIV positive, but you couldn't tell because her dark skin was still blemish-free and her body was still stacked. Keishana thought back and all she could think of was the night Taz had come to her house and started fucking her while she was asleep. God, he'd felt so good! She'd cum from his first two strokes, but when she realized what was going on, she'd hopped up and started berating him, even though he had a condom on. He calmed her down and had somehow talked her into sucking his dick with the rubber on. She wasn't going to tell them that though.

"It's been awhile," Keishana said.

"You better take on of these fine niggas, homegirl, and get that nut!" Meosha slurred, causing everybody to laugh.

"I'm straight. I got a toy at the house."

"Y'all about ready?" Kiki asked. She wanted to leave before the club ended because they hadn't brought their security teams with them and Kiki knew all the bullshit usually happened when the club let out.

They filed out of the club and made it to their cars without incident other than all the thirsty niggas trying to holler. All of them were drunk but Bella and Meosha were white boy wasted. So Kiki told Keishana to drive Meosha home and she was going to take Bella home.

"Wreck my baby shit and it's gon' be me and you," Kiki joked, but she was dead-ass serious.

Keishana rolled her eyes and did a burnout in the Ferrari just to fuck with Kiki. By the time Kiki pulled up to Bella's house, Bella had passed out. The nanny Bella had recently hired helped Bella get to her room and then left. Kiki took Bella's heels off, pulled the covers back, and rolled her into her four poster bed. Kiki worked the Gucci mini off and was about to cover Bella's naked body up when Bella grabbed her and moaned out Taz's name.

"Bella, let me go," Kiki said, snapping Bella out of her drunken stupor.

Bella's eyes snapped open. She moved her mouth as if to say something but instead she put her arms around Kiki's neck and stuck her tongue in Kiki's mouth. Kiki resisted at first, but then she got into it while they explored each other's mouths Kiki worked her mini up over her hips. They broke the kiss just long enough for Bella to pull the mini over Kiki's head. Bella sucked one of Kiki's nipples into her mouth while playing with Kiki's love button.

"Sssss!" Kiki yelled.

"Cum for me, Kiki," Bella whispered. "Pretend I'm Taz," she whispered, continuing to stroke Kiki's clit.

"Fuck!" Kiki yelled as an orgasm ripped through her body coating Bella's hand with her love juices

"Let me taste what Taz tasted," Kiki said, regaining her composure and pushing Bella back onto her back.

Kiki looked at Bella laying there and she couldn't front; Bella was a bad bitch. Bella's nipples were a shade darker than her caramel-colored skin and they poked out about an inch. Kiki flicked her tongue across Bella's nipples, causing Bella to take in a quick breath. Kiki was on a mission. She used her tongue on Bella's love box and her pussy lips peeled back like rose petals, revealing her pink insides. *I see what had Taz open over this bitch*, Kiki thought to herself, catching a whiff of Bella's intoxicating scent. Kiki sucked Bella's clit into her mouth, causing her to arch her back up all the way off the bed.

"Kiki!" Bella yelled as Kiki attacked her clit with wild abandon.

Bella locked her legs around Kiki's head as she brought her to the brink of an orgasm. It felt like it was coming from her toes. Kiki began writing Taz's name in cursive on Bella's clit and it sent her over the edge. Bella grabbed handfuls of Kiki's hair as she squirted all in Kiki's mouth. Kiki waited until Bella was done, then she climbed up Bella's body and stuck her tongue in Bella's mouth so she could taste herself.

"Where's them dildos at?" Kiki asked.

Bella couldn't answer because she was stuck on stupid from the nut she'd just got, so she nodded her head towards the nightstand by the bed.

"Yeah, bitch, got your ass stuck," said Kiki arrogantly.

Kiki got up and walked to the nightstand. She grabbed the dildo that had two ends and climbed back into the bed. Kiki positioned herself where her head was at the foot of the bed and Bella's was at the head.

"Lift your legs all the way up," she commanded Bella.

Bella did what Kiki told her and Kiki did the same so that both of their legs were in the air. Kiki reached between them and slid one end of the dildo into her.

"Shit!" Kiki yelled, relishing the feel of being stretched open.

Then Kiki scooted up and guided the other end into Bella. Bella immediately came again. Kiki put her hands on one of the poles at the end of the bed and used the leverage to push her body towards Bella, which made the dildo slide more into her and Bella at the same time so it was like they were getting fucked.

"Taz!" They yelled at the same time.

Bella saw what Kiki was doing and she put her hands on the headboard and started pushing back.

"Fuck me, Taz!" Kiki yelled out, pushing herself faster.

Every time they would push down, their clits would meet, sending what felt like electric currents through their bodies. They started pushing into each other so hard the bed started to rock. Their pussies were so wet it sounded like somebody was sucking their teeth over and over again.

"I'm about to cum!" Bella yelled.

"Me too!"

"Fuck! Fuck! Fuck!" Bella screamed as another orgasm rocked her body, which set Kiki off.

Kiki screamed, "Taz!" at the top of her lungs and started squirting. They lay there in their juices and fell asleep with the dildo still inside of them.

# Chapter 11

"Are you out of your rabbit-ass mind?" Kiki yelled into her phone.

"What? Kiki you might need to calm your ass down and watch how you talk to me!" Slick shot back.

"Or what, nigga? I told you to get your state right first! But you don't listen. You go and take it upon yourself to branch out. Did you know that the boy you killed was in the process of being OTF?" Kiki was getting more and more upset.

Kiki had called Slick to see what the hell he had going on, but the call was quickly getting out of hand.

"First off, I'm a grown man! Second off, in case you forgot, I'm not OTF so you really can't tell me what to do. Now the only reason I ain't cussed your ass out is because of my relationship with Taz, but you pushing it," Slick warned.

"Huh? Your relationship with Taz is the only reason you ain't did what? Better yet, don't answer that because you're on the verge of making me snap all the way out. Slick, get North Carolina together then try your hand elsewhere," Kiki tried reasoning with him.

"I'm good! I'm trying to really eat, and it's like you're against that."

"Say that again." Kiki got up and started pushing around her bedroom.

"You need me."

"Oh yeah? So you on your big dog shit, huh?" Kiki smirked, staring at her reflection in the mirror. "Let me remind you of a thing or two: I LET you run North Carolina! If I wasn't trying to see you eat, I'd have let one of my OTF people run the state, not you! You're starting to make me regret that decision."

"Why don't you send one of them down here to try and take it then?" Slick bossed on her and then hung up, letting his emotions get the best of him.

Kiki looked at the phone to make sure she wasn't tripping because she thought Slick had hung up on her, and sure enough, he had. She just shook her head and tossed her phone on the bed. She was going to let Slick's last comment slide because she wasn't trying to take it there with Taz's people, but when she called him in a couple days, he'd better have his mind right. Kiki didn't understand it. It's like people wanted her to get back on her rah-rah shit, but when she did, those same people would ask her why she was so aggressive. One thing Kiki had learned was that everybody respected violence!

"Fuck that!" Kiki yelled to nobody. If they wanted that dumb shit, then she was going to give it to them.

Kiki ran herself a bath. She pulled off her boy shorts and admired herself in the mirror.

"You a bad bitch," she said, grabbing a handful of her double D's. She looked and saw she had a hickey on her breast, making her think back to two nights ago. She and Bella woke up the next day after their sexcapade and busted out laughing. They talked and agreed that it wasn't going to change anything. They'd both been under a lot of stress lately and they needed it.

"Mama!" D'Angel yelled, causing Kiki to turn around and see him crawling into the room. "Mama" and "no" were his favorite two words.

"What Mommy's man doing?" Kiki picked him up, causing him to smile, showing off his only two teeth.

Kiki took his onesie off and climbed into the tub.

"Aahh!" he yelled when they hit the water, making Kiki laugh.

"Feel good, don't it?" she asked as she blew bubbles in his face.

Kiki gave them both a bath and then got out. When Kiki walked into the nursery, her nanny was dressing Damiyana, who just scowled when Kiki walked in carrying D'Angelo.

"Who you looking at like that?" Kiki scowled at her, making Damiyana's lip poke out and her eyes water, but she didn't cry.

Kiki gave D'Angelo to the nanny and picked up Damiyana. "Why are you so mean?" Kiki asked her daughter.

"Dada," Damiyana said pointing at the picture of Taz that Kiki had tattooed on her chest.

"Yes, that's our daddy, baby," Kiki said, trying not to tear up. She'd expected Taz to be here helping her raise the kids, but that wasn't going to happen.

Kiki put Damiyana in her playpen and went to get dressed. She took off her robe and put some strawberry lotion all over her body. Kiki went to her dresser and grabbed a yellow G-string with the matching bra. Then she went to her closet and pulled out a yellow and white Gucci sundress and a pair of white open toe Gucci pumps that showed off her French pedicure. Kiki put in her diamond earrings and donned a Bulgari watch, then applied some strawberry MAC to her lips.

"Where you about to go?" Meosha asked, standing in the doorway.

"Hell if I don't pray," Kiki quipped.

"Whatever," she giggled. "Did Keishana tell you about Majestic?"

"What about it?" Kiki wondered, hoping it wasn't anything bad because Taz had built Majestic Realtors from the ground up and Kiki would be damned if something was going to happen to it.

Taz had Keishana running it when he died, and that's the way Kiki had left it. Taz and Keishana had a real bond that was sealed by blood, but Kiki didn't find out until after Taz had gotten killed. She thought they had some freaky shit going on, but Kiki found out Keishana had HIV, so she knew better. But after Taz's funeral, Keishana had told Kiki that Taz had killed SK, the nigga that had given her HIV intentionally. Kiki knew that Candace, Taz's ex, was really the one that had killed SK, but she kept it to herself. Besides, Candace had killed SK for Taz, so it was all the same. Then Keishana told her that when Taz was beefing with Zion, the leader of the Zoe Pound at the time, and his son Gutta, that she'd gone to Miami and given them both HIV by fucking them both without a condom.

Keishana had turned Majestic Realtors into a powerhouse. She was selling houses at a record clip - not just any houses, but multimillion dollar houses. Taz had made her into a multimillionaire, which was another reason he and Keishana had a strong bond.

"She told me that a representative from Berkshire Hathaway home services came by the office trying to buy Majestic. And you know Berkshire Hathaway is the who's who in the luxury housing business."

"It's not for sale," Kiki said, spraying some Chanel Number 5 on her neck.

"You don't want to know the price?"

"For what? We have so much money we'll die before we can spend half of it. That's a business that generates a quarter billion annually, and it's going to stay in Taz's bloodline. He wanted to make sure his kids, kids' kids, kids' kids' kids, etc. had money," Kiki deaded the issue. Kiki made the mental note to check on Taz's other business ventures to see what was going on.

Kiki walked into the kitchen and saw Alex sitting at the bar.

"Boy, what are you doing at my house?" Kiki raised a brow.

"Uh-uh, you better leave my baby alone," Meosha said, walking into the kitchen carrying four-month-old D'Angel and stepping between Alex's legs.

"You heard her," Alex said, cuffing Meosha's ass, which was hanging out of the bottom of the Ralph Lauren boxers she had on.

Kiki shook her head and turned to reach in the refrigerator to grab a bottle of water.

"Hell no! Put her down, Alex!" Kiki said when she turned back around and saw him holding D'Angel.

"He know what he doing," Meosha tried to say.

"Alex," Kiki said in a tone that made Meosha take D'Angel back into her arms. "I understand y'all don't know no better, but if Taz was here, he'd have blanked out his mind. He didn't allow anybody to hold his girls, especially another nigga."

"I know you loved Taz and all, but damn! The nigga is dead! What the fuck he gon' do now?" Meosha said.

The nanny walked into the kitchen as Meosha was starting her little rant and as she finished, the nanny went ahead and grabbed D'Angel because she knew how Kiki was and how she felt when it came to Taz. As soon as the nanny grabbed D'Angel out of Meosha's arms, Kiki pounced. She hit Meosha with a straight jab followed by a left/right combo that caused her to fall into Alex's lap.

"Y'all, chill," Alex said, holding Meosha back from charging Kiki.

"Alex, if you don't let her go, they won't ever find all your body parts," Kiki growled through gritted teeth. The old Kiki was back!

Alex hesitated a moment before letting Meosha go. Meosha couldn't do anything with Kiki and she knew it, but her pride wasn't going to allow her to back down, especially with Alex sitting there. Meosha charged Kiki and got hit with a three-piece that dazed her. She put her head down and started swinging windmill haymakers. Kiki dodged the first two and swung a left uppercut that stood Meosha up, but Meosha connected with a haymaker that put Kiki on her ass. Seeing her chance Meosha, hopped on top of Kiki and tried to pound her out, but Kiki, being a vet, put her head in Meosha's chest so her hits weren't clean. Kiki used her hips to flip Meosha over, and it was game over. Kiki penned Meosha's arms under her knees and did damage.

"Bitch! If you ever!" POP! POP! "Disrespect!" POP! POP! "Taz again!" POP! POP! "D'Angel not gon' have a mother!" POP! POP! Kiki was fucking Meosha's pretty face up!

"Oh my God! What are y'all doing?" Bella popped up and pulled Kiki off Meosha. Bella had come to talk to Kiki and heard all the commotion.

"This slut bitch disrespected Taz!" Kiki said, out of breath.

Bella didn't say anything. She just balled her face up and looked down at a bruised and bloody Meosha.

"You better than me. I'd have killed her," Bella finally said.

Bella and Kiki walked out, leaving Alex to tend to Meosha.

to get lost before the cops got there. As Slick got in his new Challenger, his phone rang.

"Yo," he answered.

"Every time I turn around, I get a sign from you that says you're on some real live bullshit!" Kiki started up. Slick tried to say something, but Kiki cut him off. "Nah, fuck that, nigga! You got about two seconds to tell me why somebody called me, waking me up and saying that Slick was having a sit down with a motherfucker that threatened my life."

Slick looked at the phone like it had wings. "You really starting to make me feel a certain kind of way, Kiki, like I'm one of your flunkies or something."

"Motherfucker! Fuck! Your! Feelings! Nigga, why was you and Vinnie having a sit down?" Kiki amped.

Slick hung up on her and cranked his car up. He pulled out just as she called back. "What, Kiki?"

"Ha, ha, ha, ha, ha! Yo, you lucky, Slick, but your luck just ran out. If you don't tell me what you and Vinnie got going on, your brains are going to be all over the steering wheel of that pretty white Challenger you riding in," she warned.

Slick looked in the rearview mirror to see if someone was following him and almost shitted on himself. There was a nigga in his backseat with a cannon trained on him.

"So what's it gon' be?" Kiki asked, sure that Slick realized the predicament he was in.

Slick told Kiki everything involving Vinnie, including the deal Vinnie had approached him with. Kiki spared his life, but now he had to kill Vinnie.

*Nothing beats the cross but a double cross*, Kiki thought, lying back down to go to sleep.

\*\*\*

"And you say Bella and this Kiki girl have joined forces?" Big John asked.

"Yes," Vinnie said.

Vinnie couldn't get back to New York fast enough. When he did, he and his bodyguard went straight to Big John's house. It just so happened all of the dons were there having a meeting, which worked well for what Vinnie wanted to happen.

"Kiki is also the one who sanctioned the hit on Little John," Vinnie added.

"An act of war!" Alphie brought his fist down on the table.

"Can you prove this?" Anthony Franzese asked, because he knew Vinnie would tell a lie to further his cause.

"Yes. The two hoodlums are a part of her OTF crew in Baltimore. They're her muscle," Vinnie said incorrectly. Kiki was her own muscle.

"We need to weigh the pros and cons of moving against her, especially since Vinnie here says she's aligned with Bella and her Cartel," JoJo said.

"Are you serious? My first and only son is dead because of this nigger bitch! I wouldn't care if she was aligned with the President of the United States!" Big John yelled, his face turning bright red.

"If one of your kids had been killed, you wouldn't be saying a damn thing about weighing the pros and cons," Alphie said, referring to the last time someone had transgressed against JoJo and the Lucchese family.

One of JoJo's daughters and their friends had rode the subway downtown to do some shopping when they were approached by a group of boys that tried to holler at them. The girls rebuffed their advances and they took offense. After trading insults back and forth, JoJo's daughter called them some stupid niggers, which got her slapped to the floor. When she told her father, he was livid. He found out they were Crips and he waged war on them in the streets of New York. There was bloodshed on both sides for two straight weeks until eventually, Big John stepped in and ended the mini war.

"So are you guys suggesting we go to war with two crime families at once?" Tom-Tom asked, putting emphasis on the word two.

"Yes!" Alphie responded enthusiastically.

"I'm guessing you're opposed to it," JoJo said, looking over the table.

"We know Bella and her Cartel and what they're capable of, but we know nothing of this Kiki character or what she's capable of. I'm not saying revenge isn't on the agenda, but shouldn't we know who it is we're dealing with?" Tom-Tom asked.

"She's nobody! She inherited that position and her kids' father was her backbone. He's dead now, so she can be brought down," Vinnie said, trying to downplay Kiki's get down.

"Who was her kid's father?" JoJo asked.

"Taz."

"With the white-tipped dreadlocks?" Big John asked.

"Yes, do you know him?" Vinnie asked, hoping he would say no.

"I knew of him. His name was being spoken of in certain circles. He took on the Zoe Pound monkeys and the Mexican Cartel by himself. He took down the Zoe Pound and was almost successful in crippling the Mexican Cartel, but he met his ending before he could do it," Big John told them all.

"Well, he's dead, and his kids' mother is about to join him." Alphie stepped in "All in favor of taking her out, raise your hands."

Everyone agreed to the elimination of Kiki, but they weren't aware of just how deadly she was. They were about to get a lesson in warfare that many of them hadn't seen since the early days of the Mafia.

# Chapter 13

The Mafia wasted no time. They drew first blood.

Kiki had just got done with her work for the day and her security was leading her out of the building. Just as they were stepping out of the building, two vans pulled up and the side doors opened up, revealing a team of Italians. They hopped out wielding the Mafia's favorite gun, the Tommy gun. Bullets started zipping through the air at such a rapid pace that all Kiki and her security had a chance to do was get to cover. Two of the men on Kiki's security detail didn't make it. They were gunned down protecting Kiki.

"Give me a gun!" Kiki yelled as they hid behind some of the stone pillars outside of the building.

Tevin, her head security man, tossed her a .45 and Kiki started doing what she did best: slump shit! Kiki kicked her heels off and spun from around the pillar and let the .45 state its case. Her first three shots found their target. The heavy rounds of the .45 knocked one of the gunmen to the pavement. Kiki ducked back behind the pillar as all the remaining shooters focused their attention on Kiki. Her security used this as their chance to mow a few more of them down. One of the bullets from the Tommy gun knocked a piece of the pillar off, slicing Kiki's cheek.

"Fuck!" she yelled, grabbing her face

Kiki stepped back out, unloading bullets into the shooters. The Italian shooters were getting outclassed by Kiki. She'd pop out, shoot two of them, and duck back behind a different pillar. Before they realized it, they were down from twelve to four men. Not liking their odds, they retreated back to their vans and sped off.

Kiki ran over to the two security guards that had been hit to see if they were still alive, but they were dead.

"Fucking bullshit!" she yelled, bending down to close the eyes of one of her dead guards. Kiki dialed Bella's number and she answered on the first ring

"Hey girl!"

"Bella, it's war! I need you to come to Atlanta now!"

"Wait, slow down, what's going on?"

"The Mafia just sent a hit team here and they killed two members of my security team!" Kiki said, her adrenaline still pumping.

"I'm on the way right now. Give me a couple hours," Bella said, hanging up.

Kiki's next call was to Niko.

"'Sup, big homie?"

"I need you and Alex to strap up and put this work in."

"Say less. Just point the target out and we gon' make somebody mama put a dress on," Niko said confidently.

"The Italian Mafia. We're about to bring this war to their doorstep!"

"I'm about to call Alex and we gon' get on the road ASAP." Niko told her what she wanted to hear.

Next Kiki called Slick.

"Yeah," he answered.

"We about to go to war with the Mob, and I need to know right now whose side are you on. Ain't no straddling the fence."

"Is that really a question?" Slick questioned.

"Hell yeah, nigga! Have you forgotten that you were just all buddy-buddy with Vinnie, who just so happens to be a capo in the Genovese family? So?" Kiki waited for an answer.

"Yo' side, Kiki," he said, blowing air through his teeth.

"I need you and yo' team here in Atlanta yesterday!" She hung up.

They wanted a war? Well, they were going to get that and then some. Nobody was going to be safe, and that included family members. Kiki had read that there is no fate worse than to be continuously under guard because it means you are always frightened. Kiki planned on making it to where they wouldn't want to go to the bathroom by themselves.

\*\*\*

Instead of going to Atlanta to attend the meeting, Niko and Alex hopped on the interstate heading to New Jersey. Murder and mayhem was the shit they lived for. Hustling and getting money was good, but Niko and Alex loved putting in work. It was music to Niko's ears when Kiki called and said they were going to war with the Mafia. He'd read books about how the Mob gave it up back in the day, but right now, he and Alex were about to see if they could get some books written about them.

"Why you so quiet?" Niko asked his right-hand man.

"A lot on my mind, but I'm good. These Mafia niggas ain't gon' know what hit them." Alex fingered the Mac-10 laying across his lap.

"Let me find out Meosha got you gone." Niko laughed.

"Fuck outta here." He punched Niko in the arm. "But for real though, I love shorty, but she want me to move to Atlanta."

Alex dropped a bomb on Niko. Ever since he could remember, it had been him and Alex. When they had nobody, they had each other. Niko couldn't imagine running the streets of B-More Careful without his ace to watch his back.

"What you gon' do?" Niko looked over at him.

"I don't know. I ain't trying to leave you, but I don't want to lose Meosha either," he confessed.

"Go ahead down there, my nigga. It ain't like you gon' be across the country. You just gon' be a few hours away," he said, easing Alex's mind. "Now let's get ready to show these Mob motherfuckers what a real thunderstorm looks like."

As they were pulling into Newark, New Jersey, Kiki hit Niko's phone.

"What up, big homie?"

"Why y'all ain't here yet?" asked Kiki.

"Because we not coming."

"Excuse me?"

"You said we're going to war with the Mafia, correct? So me and Alex are about to do just that. We don't need to meet with everybody and go over no game plan. Most of them would probably just get in our way anyway. We got you, Kiki. You said we were going to bring the war to their doorstep, and that's what we plan to do," Niko said.

"How are you gon' do that without any help?" Kiki wondered.

"We're on the way to Anthony Franzese's house right now," he said, causing Kiki to smile.

"Handle your business then." She hung up.

Alex and Niko stopped at a gas station down the road from their destination and got out. They went to the trunk of the stolen Charger they were rigging in and put on bulletproof vests. Niko put on shoulder holsters that held twin .45's in addition to the Heckler and Koch MP10 submachine gun slung across his chest. Alex was similarly dressed, only his holsters held two Glock 30's. He had extra clips for his Mac-10 stuffed in his pockets as well as extra ammo for the Glocks.

Niko had found out Anthony Franzese's address on a humbug. Ciara, Niko's girlfriend, was friends with Anthony

Franzese's daughter Lily. Lily went to Johns Hopkins University in Baltimore with Ciara. One day she had told Ciara that her dad was a very dangerous man and that he was in the Mafia. Of course, Ciara came home and told Niko, then he found out her dad was the don of the Colombo family. He and Alex started plotting that day to hit the don. Then Lily went home for the summer and gave Ciara her parents' address. Niko and Alex couldn't find a free moment to hit him, but the time had come!

Anthony Franzese stayed on the outskirts of Newark, New Jersey in a mansion that sat on a hill. They parked on the side of the road and walked to the edge of the property at the back. It was almost 9:30 and Niko guessed that the Don was getting ready to lay down for the night. As they crept up to the house, Alex heard some growling behind him. He turned to see a teacup Chihuahua on his heels.

"Hey, puppy," he said, not wanting the dog to raise any alarms by barking.

The dog came right up to him and Alex started scratching him behind his ears.

"Peko!" A woman stuck her head out the back door and the dog took off running towards her.

Before she knew what hit her, Niko punched her in the temple, knocking her out cold. He caught her before she could hit the ground. They stepped inside, laying her down on the kitchen floor. *This is going to be easier than I thought*, Niko thought to himself.

But he was so wrong.

POW! POW! POW!

Bullets struck the wood paneling above Alex's head. He turned with the Mac-10 and sprayed a quick burst, hitting what they assumed was one of his bodyguards.

Niko ran into the living room and put a bullet in the fallen bodyguard's head as he ran past him. Niko shot the next bodyguard in the neck as he came down the hallway.

POP! POP! POP! POP! POP! POP!

The Tommy gun jumped in another of the bodyguard's hands, slamming bullets into the bulletproof vest that Niko wore, causing him to fall flat on his back.

BOOM! BOOM! BOOM!

A different one came firing from a different side of the house. Seeing his main man on the ground sent Alex into a rage. Alex let the Mac-10 rattle in his hands, mowing down both bodyguards and a third that came from upstairs.

Niko sat up, rubbing his chest. He was having a hard time breathing and his side was on fire.

"Get your shit together!" Alex said, helping Niko up.

"Man. Fuck!" Niko winced in pain as he slung his submachine gun up.

They went through the entire house until they found Anthony Franzese hiding in a walk-in closet behind his suits.

"Get your bitch ass out here!" Alex yanked him out while Niko Facetimed Kiki.

"What you want us to do with this slimeball?" Niko showed Kiki that they had the don of the Colombo family

"Damn, Anthony! My, my, my. How the tables have turned. Who all was in on putting a hit on me?" she asked

"Fuck you! You're on borrowed time. The entire five families want you dead!"

He'd answered her question, so it was war.

"And what role did Vinnie play in this?"

"You started this when you killed Vinnie's bodyguard, which just so happened to be Big John's only son." He started smiling when he saw the recognition flash across her face.

He thought it was because of it being Big John's son that was killed, but it was more so because she'd told Niko and Alex not to kill anybody. Now she had a full-blown war on her hands because of their recklessness.

"Make an example out of him, and make sure the world knows who did it." Kiki hung up.

Nicholas Lock

# Chapter 14

The Mafia dons had called an emergency meeting after Anthony Franzese's body was found in the Hudson River. The only reason they'd been able to identify his body was because of a scar on his stomach identified by his wife. They were still looking for his hands, feet, and head.

"I tried to tell you guys this was going to be a bad idea, and look what happened. One of the dons has been killed, mutilated, and dismembered," Tom-Tom said. "This is why I said we should find out who we were dealing with. I guess we know now."

"It sounds as if you're scared," Alphie said.

"I've lived a full life so I'm at peace with meeting my maker. What about you?" Tom-Tom asked, directing his gaze towards Alphie.

"We're past that now. The question now is, how do we respond?" JoJo asked.

"Send ten teams to kill her! It's that simple," Alphie said.

"I don't think it'll be that easy. Now that she knows we're trying to kill her, she's going to be on guard. It's obvious she's on a different level than what we thought," Big John said, speaking up for the first time.

"So what's the game plan?" Armando asked. He was Anthony Franzese's underboss and acting don for the Colombo family.

"The game plan is to kill her. We just have to figure out how, and I need to get Vinnie on the phone because Taz had a woman with him when he was going to war with the Mexican Cartel. If this Kiki individual is the same woman, then we're going to need to get rid of her sooner rather than later," Big John said.

"If it's that serious, we can always send Kaleetri in," JoJo said, referring to a hitman that they employed when they didn't want to get their hands dirty.

Kaleetri was their Sammy the Bull, just without the snitching. He was about forty years old and in tip top shape. He would've been a made man, but his mother was French. His killing career started when he was twelve and his mother's boyfriend at the time had decided he was going to use her as a punching bag. Kaleetri put his little sister, who was six at the time, in her room, grabbed a steak knife out of the kitchen, and stabbed him thirty times. From that day forward, he was a killing machine. He moved with his mother from Paris to New York, where he honed his killing skills by preying on the large homeless population. It was there that Big John had come into the alley behind his deli to throw out the trash and saw Kaleetri with a kid about his age against the wall with a knife stuck in his stomach. Big John saved the kid and saved Kaleetri too, because he would've eventually ended up dead or in prison with all the violence he was committing. Big John taught him the ins and outs and gave him a job as the Mafia's hitman.

"That's exactly what he need to do! Should've thought of that myself," Alphie said.

Big John sat pondering over the suggestion. The last time he'd talked to Kaleetri, he said he was semi-retired. He'd bought a house in Bridgepoint, Connecticut with his wife and two daughters, but Big John knew he could get him to kill Kiki.

"I'll call and get him on it," Big John said. "The next time we meet, it should be about the death of Kiki."

Vinnie burst into the room, thinking he'd missed the meeting, but he was arriving just in time.

"One more thing before we leave," Big John said before everyone could stand up. "It's been quite a while since we've had to do this, but we have to replace a don," Big John said, putting his head down solemnly, which was a sign to Vinnie.

Vinnie crept up behind Tom-Tom and put a garrote around his neck. He dropped his weight, nearly severing his head and spraying blood all over Alphie.

Alpine laughed, wiping the blood off his face with a napkin. "I thought you were talking about Anthony!" Alphie continued to laugh.

They made Vinnie the new don of the Bonanno/Massino family and Armando the Don of the Colombo family. They were so focused on killing Kiki that they'd forgotten about Bella.

\*\*\*

Big John was at his deli behind the counter giving a customer their order when his store suddenly filled with Hispanics. At first he thought nothing of it, but then he noticed a majority of them had crowned M's under their right eyes, a tattoo signaling membership of the Mexican Cartel. Big John told his assistant to take over for him while he went to the bathroom, but he said it so the whole store heard it. He didn't want to arouse any suspension, but he wasn't going to the bathroom. He was about to slip out the back where his bodyguards were. He made it to the back and was stepping out the back door, and then everything went black...

When Big John woke up, his hands were behind his back and his head felt like he'd gotten hit with a hammer. It wasn't a hammer. It was Quez's fist. He looked around and noticed he was in his basement. Then he noticed his wife Cathy in the corner tied to the pool table so that she was bent over the pool table. They'd caught her in bed because all she wore was a set of flannel pajamas.

"Cathy!" Big John yelled.

"Look who's awake," Bella said, stepping into his view. "We've been waiting on you to wake up." She circled him.

"Let my wife go," he said.

"She might live. All that is up to you. All you have to do is call off the hit on Kiki and give up your stake in Las Vegas."

"Are you crazy?" he yelled.

Bella backhanded him. He tried to stand up, but Drew kicked his legs out from under him and Slick kicked him in the stomach.

"No matter what you do, I'm not calling off the hit and you'll never get your hands close to Vegas," Big John said defiantly.

"We'll see," she said, walking up the steps, leaving him with Drew, Lo, Quez, Twin, Slick, and six of her soldiers, one of which was Dragon.

BOP! BOP! BOP!

Twin stole on Big John, causing him to fall to his knees.

"Just give her what she wants," Slick said.

Drew stood over him and started kicking him in the head, breaking his nose. Big John looked up at Drew and spat a glob of spit and blood in his face. Drew wiped his face and pulled his fire, but Slick stopped him. They couldn't kill him yet. Drew walked over to where his wife was and yanked her head up off the pool table.

"I'll kill you," Big John said weakly. He was on the verge of passing out.

"Tell her what she wants to hear," Slick said as Drew pulled down Cathy's pajama bottoms.

"No!" Big John yelled.

"Nah, yo, chill with that crazy shit, Drew," Slick said as Drew started to unbuckle his pants.

"Fuck this bitch! He don't want to take that hit off Kiki, so I'm about to hit his bitch," Drew said.

"Nah, yo, we not about to do that," Quez said, walking towards Drew.

But Drew pointed his gun towards the floor and let off a shot, stopping Quez. "What the fuck kind of time you on, nigga?" He mugged Drew.

"Like I said, I'm about to fuck this bitch," he said, pushing into her from behind.

"Aahh!" she cried out.

"Get the fuck off her!" Bella said, coming down the steps.

"Too late for that," Drew said, continuing to violate Big John's wife.

"I'm not gon' say it again," Bella said and her soldiers came to attention.

"You not talking about noth——"

BOOM!

Bella shot Drew in the mouth, preventing him from finishing his sentence and the rest of his life.

"Oh, you got me fucked up!" Lo swung his gun towards Bella and all the esses put their guns on him, which made Slick, Quez, and Twin point theirs at them.

"We die, you die!" Dragon yelled in broken English, the first words they'd heard him speak all day.

"Slick, you better think about who it is you have your gun on, because if you shoot me, I can guarantee you won't get a good night's rest for the rest of your life," Bella warned.

Slick looked at his niggas. They were willing to do whatever he was willing to do. But he knew their families would never be safe again.

"He was raping her." Bella threw him a lifeline.

Slick put his gun down and his crew did the same. Bella pulled on some black gloves and grabbed a golf club off a rack on the wall.

WHACK!

"Ahh!" Big John yelled from the hit to his body.

"I'm willing to beat you to death, Johnny boy, so you can make this easy on all of us by lifting the hit and signing over your stake in Vegas."

"Kiss my ass!"

WHACK! WHACK! WHACK! WHACK! WHACK!

Bella started beating him with the golf club. She didn't stop until she could barely lift her arms. Then she realized he was dead. Bella walked over to Big John's wife, stepping over Drew's body, and shot her in the head.

"Cut his head, hands, and feet off. Send his hands and feet to the other four dons. And send his head to the *New York Times* office.

While the esses went about their bloody task, Slick and Quez grabbed Drew's body and put it into their car. Bella sat back and watched as Big John was cut up. She didn't know it yet, but she'd just kicked a hornet's nest. Big John was the modern day Godfather and had love and respect with a lot of people. She and Kiki were about to have their hands full, plus Big John had unleashed a killer that wasn't going to rest until Kiki was in the dirt.

# Chapter 15

"Oh, bitch, get out of your feelings!" Kiki yelled at Meosha. They hadn't talked since the fight they'd had.

"I'm not in my feelings, I'm straight," Meosha said, but she was feeling some kind of way. She didn't like the way Kiki did her in front of Alex

"Get it off your chest" Kiki stood in the kitchen, folding her arms across her chest.

"You shouldn't have done me like that! I'm supposed to be your sister, but you treated me like a random bitch in the streets. All over a nigga that wasn't even yours!" Meosha spat, causing Kiki to clench her fists.

"You just don't get it! Taz was mine more than he was anybody else's! How many niggas you got that would die for you? Huh? And please don't say Alex, because I'm willing to put my life on it. He won't die for you. If I wanted Taz for myself, I could've had him, trust and believe that!" Kiki unclenched her fists.

"So why didn't you?"

"You're not supposed to put birds in cages, and neither are you supposed to try and chain a nigga like Taz down. Because the minute that cage opens, that bird is going to fly away and Taz is going to be like a dog with that pink thing hanging out when he gets let off the chain. When a nigga is ready to settle down, they will, but it's nothing you can do or say that's going to make a man settle down, and that includes having his baby." Kiki dropped some jewels on her sister. "Eventually we would've been together, but now that's not going to happen." Kiki burst out crying. Kiki hadn't really had time to grieve. She'd been going and going. Every time she got done with one situation, another one would pop up, which kept her busy.

"It's okay," Meosha said, hugging her twin.

With the way things were going, they were going to need each other now more than ever, and the worst had yet to come.

"Ms. Kiki, you have a call." The nanny came into the room carrying a sleeping D'Angelo.

"Oh, I got it," Kiki said.

D'Angelo woke right up when he heard his mother's voice. "Ma! Ma!" He started squirming, trying to get out of the nanny's grasp.

"Come here, boy." Kiki grabbed D'Angelo. "Hello?"

"I'm about to connect you to this call. This nigga Zeus called me," Bella said, mad as hell. "Yeah, now what you were saying?" Bella asked Zeus after connecting Kiki.

"Ya have ya son Junior. Now ya need to give mi Ares. He's not yours. Dat's Quanesha's son and his rightful place is here in da Zoe Pound."

"Not only do you have the audacity to call my phone, but you have the balls to tell me I need to give you my baby! Picture me letting you raise Taz's son. Not going to happen," Bell stated, looking over to where Ares and Junior were playing.

"Dis is not a negotiation!" Zeus yelled. "Ya in no position for another enemy! Ya can't handle da entire Mob, dere hitman, and the Zoe Pound. Mi try to give you a way to avoid dat."

"You must've bumped your fucking head! You're not getting Taz's son. The only way you'll get him is over my dead body!" Kiki said.

"If dat's da case, mi will have him real soon den." Zeus hung up.

"What hitman is he talking about?" Bella said.

"Who knows? Regardless of who he is, he'll get the same treatment as everyone else on the other side of the fence."

\*\*\*

"Mrs. Kiki, your nine o'clock appointment is here," her secretary buzzed her.

"Okay, send him in."

Kiki looked up as a tall white man stepped in her office in black slacks and a tan polo. He was average-looking with black hair and brown eyes - but Kiki had learned not to judge a book by its cover. Since coming to work in the investigation firm, she'd seen billionaires come in many different shapes, sizes, and looks. She looked over her notes and saw that he was coming to see her because he wanted this company looked into. He ran a social media site that carried millions of people's personal information and he wanted to investigate his COO.

"Hi, Mr. Fissolo. What can I do for you?" Kiki stood up and shook his hand.

"I think my COO is stealing money and I want to get out ahead of this if it's true."

"Mr. Fissolo, our rates are five thousand an hour and cases like this take a lot of time and work, so you're looking at a minimum of three hundred thousand."

"Call me Kaleetri. Mr. Fissolo makes me feel old. Money isn't an issue. Just give me the evidence I need on the bastard. You come very highly recommended, Kiki," he said, causing her antenna to go up because none of her clients used that name. They all called her Keosha.

Kiki acted as if she was going in her drawer to get some papers, but she was looking for her gun. Then she realized she'd left it in her car at lunch.

"And who was it that recommended me?" Kiki asked, taking off her red bottoms.

"Big John," he said, making the mistake of giving Kiki a warning.

Kiki threw her Starbucks mocha latte in his face and dived across her desk as Kaleetri tried to draw his gun. Kiki locked both her hands around his gun hand for dear life. Kaleetri punched Kiki in the side of her head and she nearly blacked out. She knew if she blacked out, her life was over with. Kiki used all her strength and brought her knee up into Kaleetri's balls. The gun flew out of his hand and behind the desk. Kiki tried to get to the gun, but Kaleetri snatched her hair.

"You die slow now, bitch!" Kaleetri kicked Kiki to the floor.

"You got me fucked up!" Kiki growled, kicking Kaleetri's feet from under him.

Kiki got on top of Kaleetri and started raining down blows on him. The first few landed, but he caught her wrist and turned it a way it wasn't supposed to go.

"Ah!" Kiki yelled feeling pain shoot through her body.

This is the big leagues," Kaleetri said, standing up and kicking her in the side. "You thought you were going to kill Big John, the capo di titti, and nothing was going to happen? You're lucky I got to you first because if one of the mafia dons would've got you, you'd be in for a long few days," he said, walking over and picking the gun up off the floor. Kaleetri stood over Kiki and pointed the gun between her eyes. "Tell the devil I send my regards," he said and Kiki closed her eyes.

BOOM! BOOM!

Kiki jumped at the sound of the gun, but felt no pain. She opened her eyes as Kaleetri fell to the floor. Meosha was in the doorway holding a smoking gun. She ran over to Kiki and they embraced.

"Thank you, twin," Kiki said holding her twin.

"It's all good. I was so scared," Meosha confessed.

Kiki broke the embrace and looked to where Kaleetri had fallen. All she saw was an empty space. He was gone! Kiki raced out into the hallway and there was no sign of him. Kiki had the entire building searched and no Kaleetri. It was like he'd vanished into thin air.

Nicholas Lock

# Chapter 16

Alex and Niko were in the Pork and Beans projects posted up. They were standing on the steps of another one of Niko's chicks. She was the typical hoodrat, thick, ain't good for nothing but lying on her back or getting guns in her name then reporting them stolen. Don't forget the two kids that were bad as hell. But Niko had a thing for her. Alex paid her no mind. He was focused on the apartments in front of them. Zeus was supposed to be inside and Alex had plans on sending God some company.

"You staying with me tonight?" she asked.

"Tonya, don't start that shit," Niko stated, knowing she was about to get worrisome.

"Don't start what? It's a simple question!" She stood up from between Niko's legs," Alex snapped.

"Sit your motherfucking ass down before I sit you down! You're about to blow our spot up!"

Tonya sat back down. There was something about Alex she didn't like, and she knew Niko wasn't going to be on her side if she said something. Plus she was kind've scared of Alex. He gave her the creeps.

"We about to have some action," Niko said as two silver Navigators pulled up and four Haitians pulled out. "Go ahead in the house."

She did what Niko said, seeing the look of malice in his eyes.

Alex and Nico weren't sure exactly which apartment it was, but they knew he was in one of them. As they waited for Zeus to show his face, Ciara called Niko.

"What's up, bae?" Niko answered.

"When you coming home? Curtis is teething, and I need a break," Ciara said, referring to their newborn son.

Ciara, Niko's live-in girlfriend, had been getting on him a lot lately about not spending enough time with his son. But she didn't understand the amount of things he had on his plate already. He had the whole of Baltimore under him and he was in the process of taking over all of Maryland. He'd tell her to just bear with him and in a few months, she'd be tired of him being around the house. A lot of it had to do with the fact that Niko had moved her out of Baltimore to Chevy Chase, Maryland into a five bedroom, two car garage house. The only time he'd allow her to go to B-More was for school and when he was with her. He knew niggas was playing for keeps.

"As soon as I handle this business, I'll be home."

"Okay, I love you," Ciara said.

"Love you too." Niko said.

"I know you not out here talking to no bitch!" Tonya came storming back out of the house at an inopportune time.

As Tonya was coming out of her apartment, Zeus was coming out across the street. Tonya's yelling caused Zeus to look their way and see Niko and Alex. He wasted no time leveling his .45's their way.

BOOM! BOOM! BOOM!

Zeus's first shots caught Tonya between the eyes, spraying brain matter all over Niko and Alex. Alex didn't bother to wipe her blood away. He reached down, grabbed his carbon 15, and went to work.

KAH! KAH! KAH! KAH! KAH!

Niko joined in with his SK, forcing Zeus and his comrades behind the Navigators.

TAT! TAT! TAT! TAT! TAT!

Niko was letting the SK go while walking towards the trucks.

BOOM! BOOM! BOOM! BOOM! BOOM!

A wave of Haitians came from behind them. When Niko and Alex had chosen to try and kill Zeus in the Pork and Bean projects, they didn't realize that it was a Zoe Pound stronghold. Niko and Alex were cutting them down with their assault rifles when another wave of Haitians came out of the apartments. They were outnumbered and were almost out of ammo. Niko was looking for a way out as he and Alex ducked off behind a car in the parking lot.

"We fucked up, bro," Alex said, looking over at Niko.

"Fuck it! They gon' make a movie about us," Niko said, standing up and shooting his SK.

Niko decided if he was going to die, it wasn't going to be like a coward! Niko and Alex put their backs together and went for what they knew. For every one that they shot, another three would appear.

In the midst of the chaos, Zeus had slipped away. Suddenly, four red Suburbans pulled up and a bunch of Mexican Cartel soldiers piled out. They immediately went to work on the Zoe Pound. The last Suburban pulled up to Niko and Alex and the back window rolled down, revealing Bella.

"Kiki told me what y'all had going on. And I thought I told y'all niggas that Zeus was mine," she said as her back window was shattered by a stray bullet. "Get in."

"You know we had everything under control," Alex said, getting in the back.

Bella raised her brow and looked at Alex then at Niko. "Is this true, Niko? Because I can let y'all back out." She smiled.

They both shook their heads no even though all the Zoe Pound shooters were either dead or had been run off. As much as they hated to admit it, they owed Bella their life because without her and the Cartel, they'd have been worm food.

Bella knew it too and was going to hold it over their heads in the near future.

\*\*\*

"Kiki, he won't even meet me in person no more." Slick explained to her.

Kiki was after Slick about why Vinnie's name wasn't in the obituary section yet. Since Vinnie had become one of the family dons, he'd taken to just sitting back and calling shots. What the remaining dons didn't know was that he wasn't content with just being a don; he wanted to be THE don! He was going to be the new Godfather. Vinnie felt as though the Mafia was behind the curve, that they hadn't evolved with the times. Vinnie remembered when the Mob was the most feared crime family in the States. Back then, nobody would dare oppose them. But now you had bitches like Kiki and Bella going against the grain. Vinnie had plans on bringing that fear back to the masses.

"Slick, if Taz was the one telling you to kill Vinnie, would you give him all these excuses?" Kiki inquired.

Slick thought it over and said, "Taz wouldn't ask me to kill Vinnie. He'd have done it himself."

Kiki couldn't even say anything because Slick was kind of right. Taz didn't believe in sending someone to do something he could do himself.

"Yeah, a'ight," she said and then hung up.

"What I thought," he said. "Erica, I'll be back in a minute," he told his girl.

"Bring some eggs back!" she yelled from the bedroom.

He didn't respond. He just walked out of the house. When Slick walked out, he thought it was over because the main nigga of GMC was sitting on the hood of his old school Chevy. Slick got ready to go for his pistol, but AJ shook his head.

"Yo, what's up?" Slick asked.

"That's what I'm here to figure out. Y'all niggas killed one of my little niggas and I'm trying to see how you're going to rectify this situation," AJ said, standing up to his full height of 5'11".

AJ was a terror in the city. He was with the gunplay and the fighting. Most niggas wasn't trying to fight him because of his size. He was 5'11" and 250 pounds, but he moved like someone half his size.

"To my understanding, your man pulled out first, but he wanted to shoot the clouds. AJ, you know the procedure. When you pull your gun, you use it to kill, not to scare." Slick spoke the truth AJ nodded his head in agreement.

"Is that supposed to change the fact that my mans is dead? I'll make it easy for you. This is what I need: a hundred bands and a brick. Then we'll let bygones be bygones."

*A hundred bands and a bird wasn't shit!* Slick thought to himself. He could give that up and wouldn't miss it, especially with the way South Carolina was treating him. But that was akin to extortion and even though it was a small price to pay to end all the drama, he couldn't bring himself to do it.

"Nah, my nigga, ain't nothing."

"That's what's up," AJ said, getting in his black bubble Caprice and riding off.

Slick knew that it wasn't going to end with that, but he was prepared for whatever.

He pulled out of Montebello and was riding down Cliffdale Road when a blue Challenger with dark tint pulled up alongside of him. Then a green Durango pulled up on the other side of him. By the time Slick realized what was happening, it was too late. The windows from both the Durango and the Challenger rolled down, revealing GMC niggas.

BOOM! BOOM! BOOM! BOOM! BOOM! BOOM!

They started sending shots through Slick's Chevy Nova at point blank range, but they hadn't planned on one of their shots missing. In the process of hitting Slick, the shots from the Challenger went through Slick's Nova and into the Durango, hitting the driver and one of the dudes in the backseat, killing them. Slick's car stopped and the Challenger kept going. They thought they'd killed him, but for all the shots they sent into his car, only three had hit Slick. He got hit in the arm, chest, and leg. The shot to his chest sent him into shock, which was why the car had stopped, and that was where the paramedics found him when they pulled up.

# Chapter 17

Vinnie didn't waste any time putting his stamp on the Bonanno/Massino family. He changed the name to the Giaconne family, giving the family his last name. When Big John died, Vinnie recruited a lot of his soldiers. He did the same thing with some of Anthony Franzese's soldiers, which turned Vinnie and his crew from the smallest to the largest Mafia family, and he wasn't done. He wanted to be the Mafia's governing head, but Alphie had an issue with that.

Vinnie called a meeting with the remaining dons and acting dons at his house in New Haven, Connecticut. It was a mega mansion that had ten bedrooms and six-and-a-half baths. It was enclosed with thick privacy trees that you couldn't see through and to get to the house, you had to drive up a long driveway so Vinnie and his security would see you way before you saw them. Vinnie had beefed up his security for the simple fact that he knew what the other dons didn't: that Kiki was Taz's protégé and a cold-blooded killer.

"Vinnie! You fucking schmuck! Who the fuck do you think you are?" Alphie yelled.

"Why don't we all just calm down for a minute?" JoJo said, feeling the tension building in the room.

"Calm down! This wise guy has been a don for five minutes and it already went to his head!" Alphie continued. "He thinks he can do what he pleases, but it doesn't work like that! He needs to fall in line! Then he changed the Bonanno family name to Giaconne. He didn't earn that right!"

"It's no big deal, Alphie," Armando, the current Genovese don, said. "You're the only one that seems to have an issue with it."

"That's because you idiots don't know no better! We've been doing things a certain way since the beginning."

"And that's the reason you old men need to get out of the way. It's a new generation. Everything goes through change," Vinnie finally spoke up. "Every other organization, whether it be a gang or crime family, has adapted to the new age. Everybody except the mob! This isn't the 1960's! Now is there anybody here who has a problem with me and my family being the governing body?"

"Yes!" Alphie screamed, but he was the only one to object.

Vinnie snapped his fingers and five of his bodyguards came into the room and grabbed Alphie up and took him out of the room.

"Tell Alphie's underboss Las that he's the new don of the Gambino family," Vinnie said and then looked over at JoJo.

JoJo was the only Don left of the original five. He didn't object to Vinnie being the governing body, but Vinnie knew he still had to keep an eye on him because he was the sneaky one. The Lucchese family was a powerful one with a lot of connections - connections that Vinnie needed if he was going to stay on top. Plus he knew if he killed JoJo, his underboss was his son Julian and that would start a war of the families, something Vinnie could ill-afford at the moment.

"Are you on board, JoJo?" Vinnie asked.

"Does it matter? You're going to do what you want to do anyway," he said and Vinnie narrowed his eyes.

"What does that mean?"

"Just what it sounds like. Whether or not I'm on board, you're going to do what you want regardless. I didn't raise my hand when you asked if anyone opposed you being the governing body, so that should've told you everything you needed to know. But don't for one minute think you're going to bully me into anything I don't want to do. I've been doing this for a long time, Vincent Giaconne, so keep that in mind,"

JoJo said, standing up "And make sure Alphie is able to have an open casket."

Vinnie watched as JoJo walked out, trying to decipher if JoJo had just threatened him or not.

*  *  *

"Travis where the hell is your sister?" Kiki asked.

"I ain't talked to her in a few days," he said.

"A'ight." Kiki hung up.

With Slick laid up in the hospital, Kiki had no one to run North Carolina. She thought about sending Macy to do it, but she had Tennessee to worry about. Kiki wanted Teyona to take her ass to North Carolina and run shit for about a week because Kiki thought Slick would be good by then. The hospital was keeping him for observation to make sure his leg didn't get infected. They had to operate on his thigh three times to get all the bone shards out. The doctor said he was going to have to go through months of physical therapy, but that wasn't going to deter Slick from getting some get back.

"What's up, twin?" Meosha asked.

"Shit, trying to get a hold of Teyona. You seen her?"

"Nope." She smiled and turned to walk out of the living room.

"Uh-uh, bitch, what you smiling about?" Kiki put Damiyana down and got up off the couch, pulled her boy shorts out of her butt, and followed her sister.

"You better not tell her I told you," Meosha warned, hopping up on the kitchen counter.

"Tell me what?"

"Her and Macy fucking. They been at Teyona's the last few days."

"That's why that bitch ain't been answering her phone?"

Kiki threw on a pair of khaki capris, a blue wife beater, and some blue and khaki low top Air Force 1's. The only accessories she put on were some diamond studs and some pink lip gloss.

Kiki came back out of her room and saw Meosha feeding D'Angel.

"All she do is eat," Kiki said, staring into D'Angel's silvery-white eyes.

"I know, right?" Meosha said as she pulled her breast out of D'Angel's mouth and put her on her shoulder to burp her. "Oh, and I'm about to move out too."

Kiki and Meosha had been staying at their mother's mansion in ATL together. With it being so big, it was like they had separate homes.

"Where to?"

"Buckhead. Me and Alex about to move in together. I just picked it out yesterday," Meosha said.

"If that's what you want to do." Kiki wondered what she was going to do in the mansion by herself.

Kiki kissed Damiyana and D'Angelo and left. Tevin and another one of her security people were waiting outside for her. Since her run-in with the Mafia's hitman Kaleetri, she'd been taking her security more seriously. Kiki had bought the 2021 Rolls Royce Ghost. It was cocaine white with limo tint and Kiki had it bulletproofed.

Tevin opened the back door and she slid in. Kiki rolled the partition down and gave them directions to where they were going. She pulled the shades on the back window and laid her head back. Kiki hadn't had any down time since the war had started and it was beginning to take its toll on her, physically and mentally. When everything was said and done, she was taking the twins and going on a much-needed vacation.

They pulled up to Teyona's house and got out. Kiki had a key to Teyona's house. She let herself in while her security waited outside.

"Teyona, where yo' ass at?" Kiki asked, walking through the house.

"Uh! Uh! Uh!" Teyona moaned.

Kiki peeked in the bedroom and saw Teyona on all fours with Macy fucking the shit out of her with a strap on.

"Take this dick!" Macy growled, yanking on Teyona's sew-in.

Kiki crept back out of the house. She didn't want to interrupt their fucking, but best believe they were going to hear about it and Teyona had told Kiki she didn't rock like that. Kiki got back in the Ghost and they took off back to Kiki's house. Kiki closed the shades and stretched out, relaxing until she got back home.

"What the fuck?" Kiki said when they pulled up to the house and she saw the front door wide open.

She took off into the house. "No, no, no!" she said, seeing all the shell casings.

Kiki walked in the living room and saw the nanny laid out in a pool of blood. She shot through the rest of the house, searching for her babies.

"Oh God!" she yelled, seeing Meosha curled up in the corner of the nursery.

The closer she got, the more her heart sank in her chest.

"Nooo!" she yelled, seeing the reason she was curled up.

Meosha was obviously trying to protect the babies from whoever had come into the house. Kiki moved Meosha and grabbed her babies.

Damiyana and D'Angelo were both dead.

"Why!" she cried.

"Kiki! Kiki!" her security yelled "Kiki!" Tevin grabbed her.

Kiki opened her eyes and saw Tevin looking at her. She was still in the Ghost. It was just a nightmare.

"Get me home now!"

They made a beeline for her house. Kiki hopped out and ran up to the house. She went straight to the nursery and found her babies in their playpens, which eased her mind. Kiki made her mind up right then. She had to deal with all her enemies ASAP.

# Chapter 18

"Oh my God!" Kiki said upon seeing the casino.

"I know, right? They finished way ahead of schedule. Wait until you see the inside. But check out the name," Bella said and on cue, the construction workers pulled the tarp away, revealing "The Majestic" in big blue cursive letters.

Anyone who know Taz would know that the name was memorial to him because he always would say he was majestic and he'd named his real estate company Majestic Realtors

"Come on!" Bella said excitedly, leading Kiki inside.

"Wow!" Kiki said, in awe of the building.

As soon as they walked inside the glass doors, there was a big waterfall raining down blue water. Then they were led to the casino floor. To the right was the counter where you turned your money into chips, which was behind bulletproof glass. Then to the left was the hotel check-in desk. Bella and Kiki had decided to add the hotel to the blueprint at the last minute to add to their bottom line. It was set up so that all the high rollers were picked up from the airport in one of the casino limos and brought straight to the casino. All the high roller suites had king-sized beds, hot tubs, heated floors, full bars, and free internet access, plus throughout their entire stay, all drinks were on the house.

Next they came upon rows and rows of slot machines.

"You ever played one of these?" Bella ran her hand over the lever on one of the slot machines.

"Nope. I'm not big on gambling my money. I gamble with my life on a daily basis."

"Don't I know it," Bella agreed.

They walked into the main floor, where the real gambling took place.

Blackjack tables, craps, the wheel…everything you wanted, the Majestic had it. They'd even included the hood games dookie and casualty. There was even a section that was dedicated to sports betting. It had thirty different big screen TV's showing betting lines and different games.

"Taz would've loved this," Kiki pointed out.

"You know he called himself Mr. ESPN?" Bella asked.

"So when are we going to open up?" Kiki asked, ready for her bank account to grow.

"Probably at the end of next month, because you know it's almost winter time around the world, and that means Miami's going to be brimming with money. Once word gets out that it's a casino in Miami, downtown is going to be flooded. Cha-ching!"

"That gives us about a month and a half to handle the Mafia and the Zoe Pound," Kiki said.

"It's more so Vinnie than everybody else. If we can kill him, then the other dons will probably let it go. He's the reason this whole war started."

"What about this hitman? He's a sure 'nuff problem! He handled me in my office like I was a child. I had to beef up my security for me and my house. I got about twenty OTF niggas around my house. I can't let anything happen to my babies."

"Speaking of him, I did some digging and I know where he lives with his wife and kids. Just say the word, and it's a done deal."

"Give me the address. This is personal right here."

"Have you and Meosha patched things up? Last time I saw y'all, there were punches being thrown."

"Yeah. You know she was the reason Kaleetri wasn't able to kill me in my office that day. Then we had a talk the other day, so everything is good," said Kiki.

Bella showed Kiki the rest of the casino and she fell in love with the suites. Bella told her that they had their own two personal suites on the top floor, which was the 85th floor. In total, the casino stood nine hundred feet, making it the second tallest building in Miami behind Skyrise Miami.

"Call me, girl," Bella said, walking Kiki out of the casino. "I should be done here this afternoon."

"Okay."

Kiki stood under the entranceway, waiting for her car to be brought around by her security because they didn't have the valet service set up yet. Kiki closed her eyes, enjoying the sun on her face.

"Oh, I almost forgot," Bella said coming back out of the hotel, causing Kiki to turn Bella's way.

POW!

A bullet hit the wall where Kiki's head had been. Her security surrounded her and rushed her back into the building. There weren't any more shots fired, which allowed everyone to relax. If Bella hadn't come back out and called her name, Kiki would've been dead. How many more times could she dodge death? Kiki went through her mind, wondering which one of her enemies had the skill set to take a shot at her from a distance, and only one name came to mind: Kaleetri.

***

Kaleetri was taking a day off. Kiki was turning out to either be that good or she was just the luckiest bitch on earth. Her day was coming; he was sure of that. In the meantime, he was home spending time with his wife and two teenage daughters.

"Honey, dinner's ready!" his wife yelled up the steps. "Kimberly! Desiray! You guys come eat!" she called their daughters.

They all filed down the steps with the oldest girl Kimberly coming last. She didn't want to eat because she and her boyfriend were on Facetime. These were her last few nights at home because she'd gotten accepted to Florida State University and she was leaving next week. Her mother wanted the family to spend as much time together as possible.

They'd just sat down to eat when the alarm on Kaleetri's phone went off.

"Get downstairs in the basement now!" he yelled.

"What's going on, Dad?" Kimberly asked.

"Do what I said!"

Kaleetri's home security was connected to his phone. The alarm that had gone off was the motion sensors in his backyard. When he looked at the camera on his phone, he saw a lone figure watching his house from the wood line. Kaleetri ran to his room, put his vest on, and opened his gun safe. He grabbed his custom made 45's and a M4. He was coming back out of his room when the power to the house went out. He checked his phone and saw the figure was gone. Kaleetri took the steps two at a time. He got to the first floor and stood still. He was in the blind. The only light was coming from the full moon outside. Kaleetri was trying to wait for his generator to kick in.

"How does it feel for the hunter to become the hunted?" Kiki asked from his right.

Kaleetri bent and fired in her direction, knocking pictures off the wall.

"I thought this was the big leagues," she mocked him.

Again Kaleetri fired in the direction of her voice and missed. Kiki had him off his square. Kiki had thought by bringing the fight to him, it would rattle him, and so far it was working. Everybody was good until it came time to play defense. Then she factored in that he wouldn't be able to get too reckless because his family was home. Kiki also knew she couldn't afford to play with him for too long because one slip and she would become the prey.

BOOM!

Kiki shot him in the chest, knocking the M4 out of his hands and spinning him around, but he didn't fall. The vest took the brunt of the impact, but he still felt it. Kiki's shot was a blessing and a curse because him taking the bullet spun him to the side of the room Kiki had been on. It was then that he noticed why she'd been able to locate him in the dark. The side of the living room he'd been on was bathed in moonlight.

Kiki was moving when Kaleetri let one of his .45's spit, hitting Kiki in the chest, knocking her against the wall. But what he didn't know was that Kiki had prepared herself to get shot because it was the only way she'd be able to find him in the dark. When Kaleetri's bullet slammed into Kiki's vest, his gun's spark let her know where he was. Kiki slid down the wall and sent a hot ball to the spot where the spark came from. Her aim was on point because the bullet hit Kaleetri in the same spot her first bullet did. The Desert Eagle bullet pierced the vest, this time putting a hole in his chest. Kaleetri fell back onto the sofa, grabbing his chest. Kiki had gotten to her feet and was about to step in his direction when he brought the .45 back up. Kiki jumped back and fell down the basement steps as he let the .45 talk and the generator cut on, lighting the house up.

"Dad!" Desiray screamed.

Kiki had lost her Desert Eagle in the fall. When she looked up, she saw Kaleetri's wife and daughters.

"Fuck!" Kiki said, grabbing her chest while getting to her feet.

Kiki stumbled over to where they were, grabbed Kimberly up, and put her in a choke hold. Kaleetri stumbled down the steps and saw Kiki with his oldest daughter in her grasp

"Toss your gun over here or I'll snap her neck!"

"Then what?" he asked.

"You'll probably kill me, but you'll be minus a child."

"Please, no," his wife begged.

Kaleetri knew if he gave her his gun, he was as good as dead. How did it come to this? He'd been bested by a woman! He tossed his gun at Kiki's feet.

"Pick it up and give it to me," Kiki told his wife, never taking her eyes off Kaleetri or easing the chokehold she had his daughter in.

His wife looked to Kaleetri as if asking him permission and he nodded his head. She handed Kiki the gun and she immediately put two slugs in Kaleetri's head. Kiki turned and put a bullet into each of his daughter's heads and then his wife's.

"One down, two to go," Kiki said, walking out of the house.

# Chapter 19

Once the Mafia dons heard about Kaleetri's demise, they knew things had gotten bad. JoJo reached out and got all the information he could on Kiki and OTF. JoJo and his son Julian got three of their most trusted soldiers and boarded a plane to Atlanta. They got lost three times, but they finally found Kiki's mansion.

"She's doing good for herself, eh?" JoJo said as they pulled up to her home.

"I don't know about that, Dad," Julian stated as their Denali was surrounded by armed guards

"Everybody stay calm," he told his soldiers because he saw them tensing up. "I'm here to see Kiki." JoJo rolled his window down

"And who are you?" a guard asked

"Joseph Acetturo. Don of the Lucchese crime family," he stated proudly.

The guard narrowed his eyes and spoke into his walkie-talkie. Five minutes later, Kiki came out the front door in a pink Starter jogging suit, pink Nike Shox and some pink Gucci shades. Her long hair was pulled up into a bun.

"I've never seen a zebra willingly walk into the lion's den," Kiki addressed JoJo. "And I see you brought your underboss with you," she said, letting them know she was well informed.

"We came to talk," JoJo said.

"Talk? That's funny, because a few weeks ago the only talking that y'all was trying to do involved guns. So why try to talk now? It isn't because ole Kaleetri has left this world, is it?" Kiki raised her brow and smirked.

"Honestly, no. I really just want to know how we came to this and why you put a hit on Big John's son."

"Put a hit on Big John's son? Who told you that?"

"Vinnie."

"Maybe we do have something to talk about. Come on," Kiki said, turning to walk to the house.

JoJo, his son, and his three soldiers followed Kiki inside her home.

"What about their weapons?" Tevin asked, wanting to know if he should take their guns.

"Nah, I don't take them for the type to commit suicide," she said, leading them to the office where she, her mom, her father, and Taz had their first real talk.

"You can close the door," she told Tevin, leaving Kiki alone with JoJo and his people. "Now what was you saying about me putting a hit on Big John's son?" Kiki sat down behind her big oak desk.

"Vinnie told us you placed a kill on him, but he never told us why, which was kind of funny. I mean, who would start a war for no apparent reason? I always felt like there was more to the story, so here I am."

"Okay, first and foremost, I didn't place a hit on Big John's son. Vinnie kept sending threats my way because I stopped getting drugs from him, so I sent two of my people to convince him otherwise, and one of my people was a little overzealous in sending the message," Kiki said.

"You were getting drugs from Vinnie? That's interesting, because we don't deal with drugs. The only thing Vinnie had the okay for was to find a way to get rid of Hector."

"And that's how we initially met. He gave Taz a proposition to kill Hector and he'd supply him with some work."

"So I take it the only reason you killed Big John and Anthony Franzese was because of the attempt on your life, correct?" JoJo asked and Kiki nodded her head yes. "Well,

I'm going to go back to New York and I'm going to take care of Vinnie for you. Our issues are going to be settled when I kill Vinnie." JoJo stood up and everyone followed suit.

JoJo, his son, and his soldiers left and got on the next flight out. They were walking out of the terminal when they got rushed by a swarm of FBI agents.

"How's it going, Mr. Acetturo?" Agent Edwards asked.

"I don't have anything to say and unless I'm under arrest, you need to let me by," JoJo said.

"Cuff him and them too."

"What am I under arrest for?" JoJo questioned.

"The RICO act and several conspiracies to commit murder, so even if you don't get the needle, you'll still never be a free man again." Agent Edwards smiled.

As they were putting JoJo in the back of the unmarked car, Agent Edwards leaned in and whispered in JoJo's ear, "Vinnie send his best wishes."

\*\*\*

"I'm good, nigga!" Slick said as Quez tried to help him out of the hospital. Slick's leg was in a cast, but other than that, he was good.

"Uh-uh, boy! You bringing your ass home!" Erica, Slick's girlfriend, said.

"I'll be home later." He tried to get in the truck with Quez and Twin

"Motherfucker, no! You've been in the hospital for almost two weeks! And if you think I'm going to let you leave with them, then you're crazier than I thought!" she screamed, grabbing his arm.

"Let me go, Erica."

"You know what?" she said, pulling her phone out "You need to talk to Slick! He trying to go do some dumb shit! Here." She passed him the phone.

"Who the fuck is this?" Slick amped.

"Kiki, nigga! I know you want some get back, but at least wait until you heal up," Kiki tried.

"Would you wait? Exactly!" he said when she got quiet.

Kiki wanted to get involved, but Taz fucked with some of the GMC niggas and she didn't want to go against the grain, even though Slick was also Taz's man.

"Let him get it out," Kiki told Erica when she got back on the phone.

"Ugh!" Erica yelled as she watched Slick ride off.

Quez and Twin were in the front seat of Quez's candy blue Chevy Silverado on 30's and Lo and Slick were in the back.

"Pass me that blunt," Slick said, popping a Percocet ten.

"You not gonna be demanding me, nigga," Lo said, taking another pull of the kush-filled blunt.

"Nigga!" Lo said as Slick snatched the blunt out of his mouth.

"Turn that shit up!" Slick said as Lil Baby's "Something to Prove" bumped out of the speakers.

Slick pulled the AK-47 off the floor from between his legs and laid it across his lap. They were having a welcome home party for their nigga Burn, but Slick was about to turn it into a going away party because he was about to send some niggas to meet their maker.

"Yo, I need you to set the fire alarm off so everybody can come outside," Slick told Twin as he got out.

They had parked at the Kangaroo gas station across the street from the blue building.

The fire alarm went off inside the blue building. Quez pulled out and parked in the medium strip in front of the building. Twin made it back to the truck as people started to rush out.

Slick got on the edge of the window and yelled "Get money", drawing a lot of their attention.

KAH! KAH! KAH! KAH! KAH!

Slick let the choppa do its damage.

BOOM! BOOM! BOOM! BOOM!

TAT! TAT! TAT! TAT!

Twin was sitting on the edge of the window sill shooting an AR-15 while Quez and Lo shot Glock 27's with thirty-round clips. A few of the GMC niggas tried to shoot back, but they were cut down.

"Fuck!" Slick yelled as he ran out of bullets. He took the banana clip out and threw the drum on.

KAH! KAH! KAH! KAH!

Slick sent another round of bullets at the crowd of people. Slick didn't care who got hit! He was shooting bitches and all. He was showing no remorse. They didn't show him any remorse when they'd caught him slipping.

Abruptly, Quez pulled off, burning rubber.

"What the fuck, nigga? I wasn't done!" Slick yelled.

"The police coming! Quez yelled over the music as he swerved in and out of traffic.

WOOP! WOOP! A police cruiser turned his lights on behind them.

"Not today I'm not!" Slick opened the back sliding window and let the choppa change the cop's mind about pursuing them. The 223 bullets raked across the window of the cop car, making him swerve and hit another car.

"That's how you do that!" Slick screamed as they made their getaway.

Nicholas Lock

# Chapter 20

"Damn, Meosha, you can't speak?" Niko asked and she just rolled her eyes. "What's up with your bitch?" he asked Alex.

"Bitch? You got me fucked up! Meosha screamed, getting up and walking towards Niko.

"Meosha, take your ass in the back!" Alex said, never taking his eyes off the twin Glock 19's he was cleaning.

"You're not going to say anything to him about calling me a bitch?" she asked, getting in Alex's face.

"Stop acting like on then."

"You know what? That's why he's the one in charge of Baltimore and you just second in command." Meosha walked into the bedroom.

"Yeah, yeah, whatever," Alex said to her back.

"What's her issue?" Niko asked, taking a seat across from his crime partner

"She just in her feelings about some shit she trying to do and I said no. It's bad enough she got me to move in with her, but now she thinks she about to control my life. I'm gon' fuck around and come back to B-More," Alex confessed.

"Come on then."

"We gon' see. But what's up with putting this work in?" Alex was ready to relieve some stress

"Why you think I drove all the way down here, nigga?"

Alex and Niko felt some kind of way about how Zeus and the Zoe Pound had them down bad in Pork and Bean projects., so now they were about to take a page out of Kiki's book. They were about to do the unexpected and bring the drama to Zeus, but not to just anywhere. They were about to go to Little Haiti! To many people it would be a suicide mission, but to Thunder and Lightning, it was just another day in the life of some young not giving a fuck niggas.

"Let me go get dressed," Alex said because he was wearing some balling shorts, a wife beater, and some Nike slides.

Alex walked in the bedroom and Meosha was sitting in the middle of the bed naked.

"Have you thought about what I said, baby?" Meosha asked as he went to the closet.

"I already told your black ass that that shit was a no go! If you say something else about it, I'm gon' slap the shit out of you!"

"Don't be that way, daddy," Meosha pleaded, rubbing his back. "I just want you to be the man I know you can be. Be my king," she said, putting her arms around his waist and pulling him to the bed. Meosha pulled Alex's briefs down and took him into her mouth.

"Damn, Meosha!" Alex moaned, grabbing her head.

Meosha licked around the head of his dick and cupped his balls in her hand. She jacked his dick and looked up at him. "Handle that for us, baby," she said and took him to the back of her throat.

"I got you, bae," he said, raising up on his toes.

Meosha turned into Superhead after hearing Alex say he was going to let her have her way. She started going crazy on his dick! Meosha began taking Alex all the way to the back of her throat and back to the tip over and over. Meosha was looking up at him the whole time.

Alex grabbed her ponytail and tried to slow her down, but she kept her pace up.

"Fuck!" Alex felt himself about to nut and pushed her by the forehead, making his dick come out of her mouth with a plop.

"Pussy! Let me get that nut." She tried to grab his dick, but he pushed her away.

Alex grabbed Meosha by her ponytail and spun her around so that her back was to him.

Niko pounded on the door. "Bro, I know you not in there fucking! Do that shit later! We need to get on the road," he said through the door.

"I'm coming, my nigga," Alex said, pushing into Meosha from the back.

"Ahh!" Meosha moaned out.

"Hell no, nigga!" Niko burst into the room.

When he came into the room, Alex and Meosha looked his way, but Alex kept stroking her from the back. Meosha looked Niko in the eyes and started throwing her ass back at Alex harder. Niko was stuck. Meosha looked good as fuck bent over at the waist, her titties swinging and ass clapping. Niko's dick started to rise in his Balmain jeans. Alex and Niko had an unsaid thing between them that all their hoes were game, but wifey was off limits. And Alex hadn't said whether Meosha was wifey or not. Niko looked to Alex trying to see what was up when Meosha got up on the bed on all fours. Alex didn't miss a stroke. Meosha was inviting Niko with her eyes. Niko walked to the edge of the bed and stood by Meosha's head.

"Fuck yo' pussy, nigga!" she yelled and started to rock back into Alex.

"Alex, what's good?" Niko asked with his hand on his belt.

"This pussy good, my nigga," Alex said, putting one of his legs up on the bed.

"What that mouth like though?"

"Uh! Uh! Uh!" Meosha moaned.

In the middle of her moaning, Niko pulled his dick out and started stroking it. Meosha reached out and grabbed his dick, putting it into her mouth.

"Mmm! Mmm!" she continued to moan with a mouth full of Niko's dick.

"I'm about to nut, girl!" Alex said, releasing inside of her pussy.

He pulled out grabbed him something to wear and went to hop in the shower, leaving Niko and Meosha alone. Meosha continued to give Niko head as he watched her fat ass move like it had water in it.

"Fuck that! Turn around!" Niko told her and she happily obliged. On the low, Meosha had been wanting to fuck Niko but whenever he was around, he paid her no attention.

Niko walked over to her nightstand and grabbed a jar of Vaseline and coated his dick with it.

"What you do that for? My pussy stay wet," she boasted.

"Shut the fuck up! Put your face in the pillow and put this ass up," Niko demanded.

She did what Niko said and he grabbed her ass and spread it apart. When Meosha realized what he was about to do she tried to run, but Niko grabbed her hips with one hand and used the other hand to guide his dick into her ass.

"Wait! Niko!"

"Nah, you about to take this dick," he said, easing into her inch by inch.

"Unn! Nikooo! Go slow!"

Niko got all the way in and paused. Then he began to pump in and out, making her cry out.

"FUCK! FUCK! FUCK!" Meosha cried as Niko pounded her out.

"Damn, Meosha, where you want this nut at?"

"I don't caaare!" she replied as he sped his strokes up.

Niko pulled out, went to the side of the bed where her head was, and jacked his wood until he started to shoot streams of his kids all over her face.

"I knew you was slutted out," he said, grabbing some baby wipes and cleaning himself off.

"You like it though, nigga," she said flicking his nut off her lips.

Niko shook his head and walked out to wait for Alex. He didn't have to wait long, Alex came out the back in his goon gear. He had put on a pair of black True Religion jeans, a black T-shirt, and some black Timberlands. Instead of his usual three spiked Mohawk, he just had it in one big one.

"You just had to copy me," Niko said because he had on an all-black Balmain outfit.

"Picture that. Let's go."

They hopped on the highway, heading to Miami. The whole ride all they did was listen to NBA Youngboy and pop that pink molly.

NBA Youngboy was rapping about niggas not wanting no smoke when they pulled into Little Haiti. It was almost three in the morning, but Niko and Alex were wide awake. The whole Little Haiti was going to be up when they got done. They knew Zeus's girlfriend stayed in a cul-de-sac in the middle of the hood. They had no room for slip-ups. One slip, and they'd be in the city morgue.

"It's game time, baby," Niko said as they turned onto the street she lived on. "You ready, nigga?" he asked Alex as he cocked the M-16 he had.

It was dead quiet when they got out of the green Crown Vic they were riding in. Even the crickets were quiet. They snuck up to the two story brick house, staying in the shadows. They got to the back door and Niko used the stock of the mini 14 to knock the doorknob off. Alex rushed in and went downstairs while Niko went upstairs.

"Oh my God! Oh my God!" a chocolate chick screamed and Niko slapped her with the rifle.

"Shut up, bitch! Where is Zeus?"

"He, he left about two hours ago," she cried, holding her face.

"He not here," Niko told Alex as he came into the room.

"Where the fuck he at?" Alex growled, grabbing her by the throat.

"He went to his club to handle some business." She gasped for air.

"What club?"

"Top Shotta!" she yelled, falling to the floor.

"Man, we came all the way down here for nothing!" Niko screamed, kicking her.

"Nah, we didn't," Alex said.

KAH! KAH! Alex shot Niko in the back, knocking him onto the bed. They didn't penetrate the vest, but the impact of the bullets knocked the wind out of him.

"What the fuck, bro?" Niko yelled, turning over on his back.

"It's my turn to shine! With you out of the way, I'll be the top nigga. I'm tired of being considered your little flunky. I put in just as much work as you!"

"Where the fuck is this coming from?" Niko asked, trying to sit up.

"Meosha opened my eyes to it. I can be my own boss. This is just the beginning, my nigga."

"You let that slut bitch get in your head?"

"She my slut bitch though. That's just like Ciara. She was supposed to be mine, but you got in the way."

"You know it wasn't like that, bro." Niko tried to stall so he could pull his pistol.

"Whatever it was or it wasn't, it's too late now." Alex raised his gun.

"Bro, chill!"

Alex shot Niko in the face, blowing the back of his head open. Then he shot Zeus's girl, deading her too.

Alex loved Niko to death, but their whole life he'd been in Niko's shadow. He put up with it because Niko was his right hand man and he knew it wasn't Niko's doing. It was just the way people saw them. Then Meosha put him on game. She saw the potential in him and was going to bring it out. She'd been telling him since he moved in with her that Niko was dimming his shine and all he had to do was get him out of the way, but he'd deaded the shit every time she brought it up. But before they left, something clicked and he'd seen the light. It was probably the way Niko had smirked when Meosha had said that was why Niko was in charge of Baltimore and he was just second in command.

"It's done up," Alex said into the phone.

"I knew you had it in you, daddy. Now come home and fuck your bitch," Meosha said.

"I'm on the way." He hung up.

Alex kissed Niko on what was left of his forehead and said, "I love you, my nigga." He wiped a tear away and walked out.

Nicholas Lock

# Chapter 21

"How the fuck did the shit happen?" Kiki asked.

"When I ran in the room, he was already dead and Zeus was nowhere to be found," Alex told her.

"Fuck!" She pounded the table.

"You can put Alex in Niko's spot and it'll be like it was when Niko was running Baltimore," Meosha said.

They were at Meosha and Alex's house in Buckhead and Kiki had just found out Niko had gotten killed, but she didn't know that he'd died at the hands of Alex.

"So what, you gon' move to Baltimore with him?" Kiki asked. "Because he can't run it from here in Atlanta, and furthermore, it's not just B-More anymore. We about to have the whole Maryland under us."

"I can handle it," Alex said, imagining being the king of the state.

"So you're going back to B-More?" Kiki said.

"Yes," he said.

"No," Meosha added.

"Get y'all shit together, because I got to put somebody in that spot." Kiki stood up. "I'll get back to y'all in a few days."

Kiki left the house. She needed to clear her head. Losing Niko was a blow she wasn't prepared for. She knew death came with the territory, but she'd taken a liking to the young boy. She knew Ciara was losing her mind right now. She was going to go check on her soon. And Kiki wasn't sure Alex was ready for the kind of responsibility that came with running a state. She was still trying to wrap her mind around how Zeus had gotten the drop on Niko. She'd seen Niko in the battlefield and he moved like a trained killer. Zeus was going to die a painful death for this one. Then JoJo and his son had gotten picked up by the Feds before he could run the situation down to the other dons about the scumbag shit Vinnie had going on

"Take me home," she told her security, getting in the Ghost.

Kiki had been trying to find a way to get at Vinnie, but he was on top of his game at the moment and she couldn't find an opening.

Then it popped into her head. She didn't know how she'd forgotten about it. Vinnie couldn't live without eating at the Italian restaurant The Meatball Palace in Brooklyn. Another thing Taz had taught her was that everybody had a routine. Humans are creatures of habit, whether they be good or bad. That's what had made Taz so good at robbing: because he was quick to spot his victim's habits and exploit them.

Kiki planned on making Vinnie's love of going to The Meatball Palace the death of him.

***

"Your company is here." One of Vinnie's bodyguards stuck his head in Vinnie's office/study.

"Send her to the basement," he said.

Vinnie got up and walked to the bookshelf that took up an entire wall in his office and reached up, pushing the book *The 33 Strategies of War* by Robert Greene in, and a portion of the bookshelf slid open to reveal a hidden door. He used the key he always wore around his neck to open it and disappeared down a narrow stairwell. The stairwell led to the basement.

"Hi Carmen," Vinnie said, scaring her.

"Oh my God, you scared me," she said, turning around.

Carmen was an escort from Exotic Escorts. Vinnie walked up to her and roughly grabbed one of her nipples. She didn't cry out because she knew that would make him deduct some money out of the ten thousand dollars she was going to receive for letting him have his way with her. This was her fourth time coming out to see him. Vinnie didn't usually request the same girl more than twice, but Carmen did whatever he wanted, however he wanted. Plus she was pitch black and had a perfect round butt, just the way he liked them.

"Take these clothes off and put those on," he told her, pointing to some clothes he had in the corner, which was a French maid outfit.

Vinnie had his basement turned into his own personal sex playground. He had swings, ropes, handcuffs, and whips. Whatever you could think of, Vinnie had it. And he had a secret room with a bed, a toilet, and a shower in it that was hidden by a fake brick wall. The last escort, Jalissa, had been held there for a week as Vinnie had his way with her in every way imaginable. It had cost him a hundred thousand, but it had been money well spent.

"Now get up on the table," he ordered after she put on the outfit.

It was too little for her so the shirt only covered the top portion of her ass and she couldn't button the top so her breasts were free. Vinnie slapped her on the ass as she got up on the table.

"What do you want me to do to you, Carmen?" he asked, stripping down to his birthday suit.

"I don't care," she replied coyly.

He walked around to the top of the table and rubbed his dick all over her face. Vinnie pushed into her mouth and started to move his hips back and forth.

"Take me down your throat," he said, continuing to pump in her mouth.

Carmen had to think about her father passing away to keep from laughing because he was telling her to do something that was physically impossible. Vinnie's dick didn't even reach the back of her throat, so she wasn't going to be able to do what he was asking.

"Aahh, swallow that, you black bitch!" he said, shooting off in her mouth. "Clean me off."

Carmen used her mouth to clean his dick.

"Do you want to earn some extra money?" he asked and she nodded her head yes. "You have to stay here for a week. I'll pay you fifty thousand." He shorted her because he knew there was a good chance she really needed the money.

"I have to call and tell my mom to watch my son for me," she replied.

"Okay."

Vinnie put his clothes back on and put Carmen in the secret room. She objected at first, but he told her he'd give her an extra fifteen thousand and she agreed.

"Bring the car around. I'm hungry" he told one of the bodyguards.

"Put this on." He tried to hand Vinnie a vest.

"We're just going to The Meatball Palace," he said, bypassing the vest. Vinnie walked outside and got in his 2020 stretch Navigator, which was custom-made by Luxury Sales in L.A. It was fully loaded and bulletproof.

The ride to New York was one of comfort. He reclined and watched his favorite movie, *The Godfather*. In his mind he was the father of Michael and Sonny.

"We're here, boss," his guards spoke into the intercom.

They got out first and checked the inside of the restaurant before allowing Vinnie to come in. Satisfied, they opened the door to let Vinnie out of the limo. He went to the table he sat at every time he came through: the back table. His guards positioned themselves by the door and at the bar. Vinnie felt as if he was untouchable. He'd gotten Joseph Acetturo out of the way and put one of JoJo's capos in charge of the Lucchese family that was sympathetic to his cause. If only Agent Edwards would take care of Kiki and Bella, he'd be on top of the world.

"Here's your order, Vinnie." The owner brought him his order.

"Thanks, Sonny."

Just as Vinnie was about to dig in, the restaurant door opened up and a group of kids came in arguing about a basketball game.

"I like your limo," one of the kids said to Vinnie.

"Thanks, kid. Hey wait a minute, how did you know the limo was mine?" Vinnie asked because they weren't out there when he pulled up.

"Her." One of the kids pointed towards the back by the bathrooms.

BOOM! BOOM! BOOM! BOOM!

Kiki shot both of Vinnie's bodyguards. She hit one in the neck and the other one got hit in his left ear.

"Get your ass up!" Kiki yanked Vinnie up by his shirt. "Come on." She dragged him to the front of the restaurant.

KABOOM!

The owner shot Kiki in the chest with a sawed off, knocking her through the glass door. Kiki started clawing at her vest, trying to breathe, because she'd had the wind knocked out of her. The level four military vest had stopped the shotgun slugs.

The owner stepped out the door and was bringing the shotgun back up when Kiki shot him in the face. When Kiki finally regained her senses, Vinnie had gotten low. With sirens in the distance, she didn't have time to go looking for him.

Kiki disappeared down an alley, mad at herself, because she knew she'd just blown a golden opportunity.

# Chapter 22

"The big bad Kiki all hurt up. I thought you was Superwoman," Travis joked.

"Travis, shut up!" Teyona told her brother.

They had gathered at Kiki's house. Kiki was laid up on the couch with her midsection wrapped in an Ace bandage. The shotgun slugs struck the vest with so much force that they had broken five of her ribs. Every time she took a breath, a sharp pain would shoot through her side. It had gotten to the point where she was trying to limit her breaths.

"I'm glad to know you're in such a jolly mood because with me laid up, you're going to be on the front line now," Kiki told Travis.

"Don't look like that!" Teyona laughed, seeing the look on his face.

"Oh, you thought you were just going to be around here living the good life and not have to get your hands dirty? News flash! It's a war going on and whether you realize it or not, you're in it," Kiki broke it down for him.

"What exactly are you expecting me to do?" he asked, making Kiki look to Teyona with a crazy look on her face.

"Bust! Your! Fucking! Gun!" Kiki screamed, sending pain all through her side. "You too, Teyona, ain't no more free rides. I been carrying this OTF shit since my mama died. Y'all about to pull y'all's weight."

"Go ahead and get better, twin, I got you," Meosha finally spoke up.

"You got me? What you gon' do?"

"Run OTF until you get back right," she said.

"I'm all right right now! If motherfuckers think a few broke ribs is going to stop me, then it's obvious they don't know me. My trigga finger still work - both of them! Even if they weren't I'd shoot with my feet! Yeah! Kiki is all the way like that! Matter of fact, Teyona, call everybody up and tell them to be here tomorrow. We need to have a meeting." Kiki threw her weight around. "And when you get done with that, I got to holler at you," she said to Teyona. Kiki got up and walked to her room. D'Angel woke up as soon as she walked in.

"What you doing, man? I'm not picking you up," she told him as he reached his hands for her.

Kiki sat down on the bed and he crawled into her lap. Damiyana and D'Angelo were a year old now and were getting into everything. Neither Kiki nor the nanny could take their eyes off of them for a minute or they'd get into something. The two of them learning how to crawl had turned out to be a headache.

"What you want, girl?" Teyona asked, stepping into the room.

"What's up with you and Macy?"

"Nothing," she said, picking Damiyana up, who had just woken up too.

"So y'all not doing it?" Kiki asked, not wanting to say fucking in front of the twins.

"Girl, no!"

"So you're going to lie in my face? I walked in your house the other week and I saw Macy dragging you from the back. Now say I'm lying," Kiki dared.

"It was a one-time thing, okay? Don't be trying to judge me," Teyona said, about to lose her cool.

"Judge you? I just asked a question and you got all defensive *after* you lied. You're basically my second-in-command, so I need to be able to trust you. If you'll lie to me, you'll steal from me, Teyona. I love you, but stealing from me will get you the death penalty." Kiki gazed at her with her grey eyes.

"I got you——"

Kiki cut her off. "Don't tell me; show me. Actions speak louder than words."

Teyona nodded her head and left with Kiki's words ringing in her head.

*** 

"Everybody here is OTF with the exception of Slick and his crew, and they're an extension of us. But the reason I called you all here today is because as you know we're at war with the Mafia and the Zoe Pound Mafia," Kiki said from the balcony overlooking her living room.

There was close to a hundred people in her living room. And this wasn't close to the whole OTF team.

"This is how it's going down from now on. Any Mafia or Zoe Pound motherfucker you see, it's gun smoke, straight like that. We need to put an end to this once and for all! I'm tired of being the only one getting my hands dirty."

"My gun blow like your gun blow! You not the only one putting on for the team," Alex said from the back of the room.

Kiki looked at him and had to bite back a slick remark. This was the exact reason she was skeptical about putting him in charge of Maryland. Kiki wasn't going to blank - at least not yet.

"Gangstas move in silence. They don't like their exploits made known. Only insecure niggas and niggas trying to prove something brag about what they've done or what they will do," Kiki said. She couldn't help herself. She had to say something. "I expect everyone to handle their business as usual, but if the death toll don't rise among Haitians and Italians in y'all's cities, it's something wrong."

"What about us that live in cities where there ain't no Zoe Pound or Mafia presence?" Macy asked.

"I'm really directing my voice at the people in Miami, North Carolina, and Maryland. Because we're just focusing on the New York families as far as the Mafia is concerned. Another reason I brought everyone here is because I have some new product for us. It's nothing you haven't heard of. We just haven't dealt with it."

"What is it?" Slick asked.

"Damn, let me finish." Kiki grinned. "This right here is going to make all of you millionaires." She held up what looked like clear glass. "It's crystal meth."

"That's wild, because I just had some people asking for that," Slick said.

"Before y'all leave, talk to Teyona and Travis and they're going to get you straight."

"Let me holler at you before I leave, Kiki," Macy said.

Kiki came downstairs and pulled Macy into her office. "What up?"

"I have some dudes you should meet. I've been supplying them for a while now and every time they come, they get more than what they got the last time. Plus I know you want OTF in different cities."

"Who are they?" Macy had her attention.

"It's different dudes. First there's Flip from Virginia, there's Body from Kentucky, Justin from Alabama, then it's these two Gangsta Disciples from Chicago named Anthony and Akira. They're brother and sister."

"I'll meet them, but if they turn out to be some bullshit, it's on you, Macy."

"Got you. I'ma set it up for them to come down here to you."

"Make it happen. Now bye." Kiki was tired and she wanted to spend some time with her twins.

# Chapter 23

Bella had been focusing all her energy on getting the casino up and running. She hadn't had any time to put Zeus in his proper place: a closed casket. Everything was ready to go with the casino. All she had to do now was set a grand opening date. That was something she and Kiki had to collaborate on. She needed to get on her job because Kiki had been on hers. Kiki had knocked the Mafia's hitman off and was giving the Mafia all they could handle. It was time for Bella to give the Zoe Pound the business.

Things were about to be different now. Bella had proved to her Cartel that she was more than willing to put in work. From now on, though, she was just going to sit back and call the shots. She was more important to them alive. Bella had tried to tell Kiki to take a backseat as far as putting in work and being on the frontline, but she wouldn't listen. Kiki's pussy got wet from busting her gun and Bella kind of understood because Kiki came up beside Taz putting in work, so it was almost like it was her first love. Bella, on the other hand, came up not having to break a nail, so it was going to be easier for her to sit back, give orders, and play with her babies. Junior was two years old now and was coming into himself. Ares was one and a half and he was a handful. Anything he could get into, he did. Eve was only four months old, so she was the easiest one to deal with.

Bella had learned from Kiki that Zeus owned the nightclub Top Shottas in Miami. Lately she'd been seeing flyers around advertising a party at the club. There was supposed to be a popular Jamaican artist coming to perform his hit song, so the club was going to be jam-packed. Bella had Dragon flown in from Mexico and he was going to be the one leading the assault. Tonight, Zeus was going to meet his maker, and Bella was sure of that.

She wrapped things up and called down and told her security team. She was about to leave for the day. Kiki had called her and told her to go check on Taz's businesses to see how things were going. Bella walked out of the casino and her sunburst gold Bentley Flying Spur was waiting for her. She got in the back while two of her security guards got up front. Bella looked behind her and saw a black Range Rover that held four more of her personal security detail. Their first stop was Primo's Pizza, one of the businesses Taz had saved from financial troubles and bought into. Bella talked to Johnny, the co-owner and he told her everything was good. Next she went by the Wiener Works office where she met with Victoria. Weiner Works was owned by Victoria and her sister Olivia, but Taz had a percentage of the business. Taz also had a personal relationship with Victoria, something Bella didn't know about. As with Primo's Pizza, everything was on the up and up. Weiner Works had just been featured on the cover of *Entrepreneur* magazine as the next McDonald's. Her last step was Majestic Realtors, Taz's real estate company.

"Hey girl!" Keishana said when Bella walked in. They hugged and she led Bella to her office. "What brings you here?" Keishana asked.

"Kiki wanted me to see how things were going," she said, sitting down.

"Girl, you look like you getting thicker too," Bella pointed out.

Keishana was wearing some white Chanel pants and a white Chanel blouse, but it looked like she'd been born in the pants. Then with her being dark chocolate, the contrast between her skin and the white outfit made quite the picture.

"I been gaining weight. It's this new medicine they have me on," she said happily. "The doctor says this medicine will allow me to have sex and not pass the virus. He said I have to wait six months, then everything will be a go."

"Oh God! You ain't gon' know how to act." Bella smiled.

"Okayyy!" They high-fived.

"So everything is good?"

"Is it? Did you see that old white man that was walking out as you were coming in? Boca Raton; that hit his wallet for 8.9 million dollars! Now you tell me, is everything good?"

"Oh my God! Is that why your blouse is undone so low?" Bella joked.

"Oops." She buttoned up the top two buttons. "Girl, you show these old white men a little skin and you basically write your own check."

"Aw, man, how you doing, sexy?" a tall, dark-skinned man walked into Keishana's office and asked Bella.

"Better than you," she said, turning back towards Keishana.

"Don't be like that. My name Chris." He stuck his hand out

"Isabella," she said, shaking his hand. "Now excuse you."

"Not until I get your number."

"I'm married."

"Where's your wedding ring then?" He kept at it.

"It's getting cleaned."

Keishana was about to shoo Chris off, but she was enjoying the verbal sparring match she was witnessing.

"And your husband is okay with that?"

"What he wouldn't be okay with is me talking to you."

"He must be insecure as hell then," he said, starting to tread in dangerous waters.

Keishana saw Bella stiffen up with his last statement. She started to say something, but Bella beat her to it.

"You were doing halfway decent until your last statement. Let me school you real quick. When you're attempting to holler at a woman, NEVER try to use their man to further your efforts. It makes you look inferior. Like maybe you have an insecurity," Bella gave him some jewels. "And my husband is deceased."

"I'm sorry," he said. "Does that mean I can't get your number?"

"Look, Chris, you seem like an okay guy and all, but dealing with me is liable to bring you problems. Problems that I'm more than sure you're ill-equipped to handle."

"Give me your number and we'll cross that road when the time comes," he said.

"Remember that you did this to yourself." Bella wrote her number on his hand.

"Now go do some work, Chris." Keishana shooed him away.

"He's a cutie," Bella said.

Keishana didn't respond immediately because she was unsure of what to say. It felt like she was going against the grain by allowing Bella to entertain Chris. At first she thought Bella was just playing with him, but when she gave him her number, all that changed.

"Are you sure about this, Bella?" Keishana questioned.

"Relax, girl, I'm just going to tease him a little bit."

"Oh, okay." She breathed a sigh of relief,

"Let me get out of here. Tonight is going to be a good night."

"Why you say that?" she wondered.

"Watch the news," Bella said and then walked out.

As Bella was walking out, she saw Chris watching her out the corner of her eye so she put a little extra rock in her hips. She was sure she saw him grab his dick before she walked out.

\*\*\*

Top Shottas was right down the road from Little Haiti, but Bella didn't care. She wanted blood. She wasn't going to actively participate, but she wasn't going to sit at home and twiddle her thumbs either. Bella was going to watch everything take place from a safe distance. Top Shottas wasn't little, but it wasn't big either. Top Shottas held about two thousand people. These two thousand people were going to be mainly Zoe Pound because it was a Haitian club and all they played was reggae music. Everyone in Miami knew Top Shottas was where the Zoe Pound partied at, so Bella wasn't going to feel sorry for anyone tonight.

Dragon waited until eleven-thirty when he was sure the club would be packed. He barred the back door so no one could get out that way. There were a total of twenty-five Mexican Cartel members accompanying Dragon, and all of them were hardened killers. A lot of them carried machetes as their weapon of choice. The bouncers had gone inside so there wasn't anybody to try and stop them as all twenty-five esses rushed inside the club. The bouncers were the first to get cut down. The machetes that some of the Cartel members were wielding were so sharp that they were cutting all the way through the bone. Two of the bouncers had their arms sliced in half.

BOOM! BOOM! BOOM! BOOM!

The rest of the esses had handguns and assault rifles. The gunshots sent the club into a frenzy. People started rushing to the door, only to run into their deaths.

The assault rifles were splitting people in half and the Cartel was showing no mercy. They were shooting women and all. When the club patrons saw that the front door was a death trap, they ran to the back door, which was what Dragon was anticipating, and that was why he'd barred the door. Dragon went to find Zeus while the rest of the Cartel members mowed down everyone else. He found the office on the second floor, but there was no sign of Zeus. Dragon was about to walk back out when he noticed a side door. Fearing Zeus was going to escape, he burst through it. He found himself on a balcony outside with steps leading out the back. At the bottom, he saw Zeus and two other Zoe Pounds getting into a yellow Charger.

Dragon sent four shots from his Sig Sauer .40, busting the back window out. Zeus was able to get in the Charger and pull out.

Bella and her security were across the street parked in her G-wagon, waiting to see the outcome, when she heard the shots.

"Pull around the back," she ordered.

When they pulled around the back, a yellow Charger shot past them. Bella saw Dragon standing on top of a balcony with his gun in his hand. When he saw the G-wagon, he pointed towards the Charger.

"Catch that Charger!" Bella yelled and her security whipped around, trying to do as they were told.

Bella had wanted to avoid participating, but it looked like that wasn't going to happen. She reached behind her, grabbed the mini 14 off the floor, and rolled the back window down. Whoever was driving the Charger had slowed down after getting away from the club. Otherwise, they'd have never caught up to them

"Get up alongside them," Bella said.

Just as they got on the SW Avenue Bridge, Bella leaned out the window and let the mini 14 spit.

Bullets raked along the side of the Charger. The Charger bounced off the car next to it and hit the guard rail, flipping it over the rail and into the water. They rode back by Top Shottas and the whole building was up in flames. Bella would sleep well tonight. Another one down with one left to go.

Nicholas Lock

# Chapter 24

Kiki was at her house waiting for Macy to show up with the people she wanted Kiki to meet. Kiki wanted to have an OTF presence in every state and was in the process of making it happen, but then the war happened.

Macy finally showed up and Kiki looked them all over. The nigga Body from Kentucky was brown-skinned, heavyset, and had a brush cut that had designs cut on the sides. Then there was Flip from VA and he was dark-skinned and rocked the Mad Max. He had dreads on top, but the sides were shaved bald and he was toothpick skinny. The Alabama nigga Justin was the tallest person Kiki had ever seen in person. He was seven feet tall with dreads that hung almost to the floor. When he sat down, he had to tuck his dreads in his pocket. He was originally from Sierra Leone. He'd come to the U.S. when he was sixteen with his mother. Now at twenty-one, he'd been in the States for five years. Out of the five, Justin was the most ruthless. It came from growing up in the slums of Africa. Then there were the siblings, Anthony and Akira. Akira was eighteen and Anthony was twenty. They were both high yellow with long hair. Anthony's hair was done in box braids and Akira's was done in two French braids. Both of their hair fell to the middle of their backs. Akira had a black bandana around her head and Anthony had one around his right wrist, signaling their Gangsta Disciple membership.

"I'm pretty sure everyone knows why they're here, but I need to be sold on why I should deal with you," Kiki said.

Justin was the first one to speak up. "Alabama runs through me. I supply a majority of my state and with you in my corner, I'd be able to solidify that spot. And at the same time, you'd gain another state and a crew full of hungry wolves and go-getters," he said.

Kiki had to really listen to him because his accent was so thick.

Flip was next up to speak. "Not only can I bring you Virginia, but I can bring you West Virginia too, and you know West Virginia is ninety-three percent white. And they love crystal meth and powder."

Body caught Kiki by surprise when he started talking because for him to be heavyset, he had a small voice. He sounded like Mike Tyson.

"Yo, my résumé speaks for itself. I took Kentucky from the last three niggas that was holding it down and I did it by myself. I earned my name and my stripes, plus my hustle game is like nothing the world has ever seen before. I was the first nigga in my state with a Phantom."

Kiki liked him. He reminded her of Reggie with his big boy swag.

"So y'all saved the best for last," Anthony started up "I can't say we run Chicago because no one holds that position, but in GD we hold weight. With us on the team, you'll have an army of niggas that don't mind getting their hands dirty and chase that bag."

"And we're not just in Chicago. That's just our headquarters. Every state that was just named, we have homies there whether you know it or not, and that includes Georgia, Florida, South and North Carolina, and beyond. I dare one of you to say I'm lying," Akira said.

Kiki looked around and everyone nodded, so it was the truth. Akira was a little rough around the edges, but Kiki could see the potential in her. With Kiki's guidance, she'd be a criminal.

"From this day forth, your beef is mine and vice versa. Whatever you need as far as work, talk to Teyona or Travis and they'll get you straight. Tonight we're going to the club to celebrate our business partnership."

As they were all making their way out and to their cars, ten black SUV's pulled up. Agent Edwards got out of the lead truck and walked right up to Kiki.

"Going somewhere?" he asked Kiki.

"About my business. What are you doing at my home?"

"You need to come with me and you can come willingly or in handcuffs, it doesn't matter to me."

"Call the lawyer," Kiki told Teyona as she was led away.

The whole ride to wherever they were taking her, Kiki was trying to figure out if she'd slipped up somewhere or not. But she knew she'd been extra careful. Nobody could identify her in any of her situations. She wasn't in cuffs, so they couldn't have anything concrete.

They pulled up to the federal building downtown and escorted Kiki inside. The whole walk, Kiki held her head high. She wasn't gon' let them see her sweat. Agent Edwards put her in an interrogation room and cuffed her to the chair. Kiki knew the game; Taz had schooled her. They were going to leave her in the room for a few hours to break her down then try to get her to confess, but they were in for a rude awakening. She stretched her legs out and took a nap.

Finally, Agent Edwards came into the room, slammed the door, and threw some pictures on the table.

"Tell me what all these pictures have in common?" he asked, pushing them her way.

Kiki's heart dropped. He had pictures of her in the catsuit leaving Juan's house the night she killed him. There were pictures of her outside the Mafia hitman Kaleetri's house and he had pictures of her at The Meatball Palace the day she'd tried to kill Vinnie. The last few pictures were of her and Taz at the funeral home when they killed Zion. She was fucked.

But the more she looked at them, the more she realized that you couldn't really see her face. They were all either too distorted or the angle only showed her silhouette.

"I don't know, you tell me." She slid them back across the table

"Okay, smart ass! They're all you!"

"Nice try; wrong guy. Not one of those pictures show the person's face for all I know them could be pictures of you" Kiki said smugly

"You think this is a game, Keosha?" he yelled, using her government name. "I can have you charged with numerous murders, money laundering, and the RICO act!" He got in her face.

"I'm ready when you are. What's taking so long?" Kiki tested him.

"When I get you, I want to get Isabella Vasquez as well. That way y'all can share a cell for the rest of your miserable lives. I want your kids to grow up without their parents, just like the kids of all the people you've killed."

"Ohhh, somebody's taking this personal. You know you shouldn't involve your personal feelings in your job," Kiki started fucking with him.

"See how personal you take it when someone else is raising your kids while you rot in the Federal penitentiary"

"I see you like bringing my children up. Do you have kids, Agent Edwards? If so, being that you claim to know me and what I'm capable of, you can't love them." Kiki was starting to get mad.

"Why would you say that?"

"Keep doing what you're doing and you'll find out."

"Are you threatening a Federal agent?"

Kiki's lawyer burst into the interrogation room. "If my client isn't under arrest, then she needs to be released right now," her lawyer said.

Ten minutes later, Kiki was walking out of the building a free woman. She looked back and saw Edwards watching her. He'd exposed his hand. Now it was time for Kiki to show him her royal flush.

Nicholas Lock

# Chapter 25

After Kiki told Bella about her run-in with Agent Edwards and how he said he wanted Bella too, she went to work. Her dad had contacts all over the globe and in different agencies. She put them to use. Bella started gathering all the information she could on Agent Edwards. All the intel she gathered indicated that he was a bulldog. Once he set his sights on someone, he brought them in. But he hadn't encountered anybody like Bella and Kiki.

Agent Edwards had graduated at the top of his class at Quantico. He started out working in the fraud department and excelled. He moved up the ladder at a rapid pace. Within five years, he was put in charge of the organized crime unit. Since then, he'd turned numerous high-ranking members of organized crime families into government informants. In return, Edwards allowed them to continue their illegal activities and he got monetary compensation. Vinnie was the last person he'd turned. Agent Edwards had caught Vinnie on a wiretap discussing a murder plot and from that day forth, Vinnie had been a federal informant.

The most valuable information that Bella had gotten out of her contact was Agent Edward's home address.

"Guess whose address I have on my desk?" Bella asked Kiki.

"Who?"

"Agent Edwards."

"Text me that shit ASAP. I got a trick for his ass," Kiki said, putting together a plan in her head.

"What you got up your sleeve?" asked Bella. "Better yet, I don't want to know, but whatever it is, make sure it's done right," she gave Kiki some advice.

"This me you talking to."

"Okay, okay, go ahead and do your thing," Bella said and then hung up.

Bella massaged her temples because she felt a migraine coming.

"Ma-Ma," Junior said, running into her room.

"What's up, boy?" She picked him up.

"Eat, eat!" he yelled, causing her to laugh.

Junior was acting more and more like Taz every day. He was even developing Taz's mean streak. More than once over the last week she'd had to separate him and Ares because Junior was being mean to him. He'd taken after Taz with his feelings towards women because he adored his little sister Eve. Whenever she would start to cry, Junior would run and try to give her a bottle or her pacifier.

Bella carried Junior into the kitchen and made him a peanut butter sandwich. While he ate, Bella got herself ready to go to the casino. She took her hair out of the ponytail and let it fall. It still fell to her ass.

"I got to hit the salon," Bella said out loud, seeing that the blond highlights in her hair had started to fade.

Bella looked in her closet and pulled out some white Prada capris, a pink Prada T-shirt and some pink Prada open toe sandals. She finished the outfit with a necklace that had her name in it in diamonds and some white Prada shades.

"Hello?" Bella answered the phone when it rang.

"What's going on, sexy?" a strange voice asked.

"Who is this?"

"Chris."

"Oh, hey!" she said, smiling.

"Are you busy today? Because if not, I'd love to take you out to this new steakhouse."

"And what time would that be?" Bella asked, turning to the side to see how her butt looked in the capris.

"Right now. You dressed?"

"Tell me where the new steakhouse is and I'll meet you there."

Chris gave her the address and hung up

"What am I doing?" Bella asked the mirror.

Was this a date? Hell no! Bella didn't know what she was doing by going out with Chris. She wasn't trying to move on from Taz, but he'd been gone for a while now and she knew he'd want her to live her life. But could she really see herself with someone else? She found herself comparing Chris to Taz and there was really no comparison. Bella was just going to have a little bit of fun with him and send him about his business.

"Ms. Barbara, I'll be back later on," Bella told the nanny. "I'm good. I won't be gone long," she told her security as they tried to get up and go with her.

Bella put her .380 in her purse and got in her G-wagon. She pulled up to the steakhouse twenty minutes later and walked inside. Chris had a table in the back, he pulled her chair out for her when she walked up.

"Thank you," she said.

Bella looked Chris over and nodded her head in approval. He was wearing a pink Ralph Lauren Polo, some white Levi's, and some pink and white Foamposites. The only jewelry he wore was a white G-shock.

"Great minds think alike," Chris said pointing at their matching outfits.

Bella rolled her eyes. "What are you having?" Bella looked over the menu.

"Whatever you are," he said, making her look up.

Bella waved the waiter over and ordered two steaks well done and a stuffed bell pepper.

"So how long have you been working at Majestic Realtors?"

"About seven months," he said, staring at her.

"Do you like it?"

"Of course! I make too much money not to," he bragged.

"But what do you do for a living?"

"I own an import/export business, and have you seen the casino downtown? Well, I own that with my sister."

"Who hasn't seen it? It's the talk of the city! I heard it's going to open in two weeks."

"Yup, so make sure you come spend some money with us."

"I'm trying to spend more than money with you. I'm trying to spend some quality time with you."

He was saying all the right things. It had been a long time since Bella had had a man talk to her like this.

"What kind of car do you drive?"

"I got the new Navigator."

"Good, come on." Bella grabbed his hand and pulled him up.

Bella didn't know what had gotten into her, but her pussy was on fire! They got into the back of his Navigator and laid the seats down.

"Suck this pussy!" Bella said, taking her capris off, showing Chris she didn't have on any panties.

"Mmm-hmm," Bella moaned as Chris sucked her clit into his mouth.

Chris ran his tongue up and down her slit while pushing two fingers inside her pussy. He knew by how tight her pussy gripped his fingers that she wasn't getting fucked on the regular.

"Hell yesss," she moaned. "Don't stop!" Bella could feel an orgasm coming.

Chris kept eating Bella's pussy and was rewarded with a face full of her juices. He sucked up every drop. Bella was the baddest chick he'd ever fucked, plus she had that bag, so he was pulling out all the stops.

"How does it taste?" she asked, looking down at him.

"Like sugar," he said, pulling his pants down.

"Uh-uh! Where your condom?" Bella pushed him away before he could put his dick in her.

"I'm gon' pull out."

"Get a condom," she said seriously.

Chris reached in his pocket, pulled a Trojan extra sensitive out, and slid it on.

"Oh shit!" Chris said, feeling the way her pussy was holding his dick. He started rocking into Bella, making her scratch his back up.

"Don't play with it! Fuck this pussy!" She threw her legs up so he could go deeper.

"This my pussy!" he panted, hitting her spot. "Say it! Say this my pussy!" Chris growled, trying to tear her walls down.

"Un! Un! Un! Un! Fuuuck!" Bella moaned.

"Say this my pussy, Bella!" he said, putting her legs over his shoulders.

"No, nigga! Just fuck me and shut up!" She matched him stroke for stroke.

"I got something for your ass!" Chris flipped her over and mushed her head into the carpet.

As he was pushing into her, he saw the name Taz across the lower part of her back with hearts around it. Then on her left cheek she had the Tasmanian devil pointing two pistols at him and on the other cheek it was the Tasmanian devil holding his middle fingers up.

Chris smacked her ass and tried to dig her guts out. "Whose pussy is this?"

"Just fuck me, nigga!" Bella used her hands to push back into him.

"I'm about to nut. Turn over."

Bella turned over, thinking he was about to go back inside her, but he pulled the condom off and started jacking his dick. The first shot hit her on the stomach, but the next one landed on her face.

"I should fuck you up!" she said, grabbing his shirt and wiping herself off.

"Damn, my bad," he said.

"Whatever." Bella put her capris back on.

Bella was already feeling guilty about fucking him. She had to get out of the truck. Bella was about to open the door when a familiar face caught her eye.

"Ain't no way! How many lives do this pussy got?"

Bella wanted to shoot him, but there were too many people with him. Fuck! This was a major problem because Zeus wasn't dead.

# Chapter 26

One monkey didn't stop no show! Bella and Kiki had to keep things moving with the casino. Today was the grand opening of The Majestic and all the who's-who were in attendance. Even the owners of the casinos in Las Vegas showed up. The grand opening was turning out to be the biggest event of the year.

"Oh my God, girl, there go Denzel Washington!" Bella pointed him out to Kiki.

"Girl, act like you been somewhere before." Kiki nudged her in the ribs.

Bella and Kiki looked the part of casino owners. Kiki was wearing a custom made white Herve Leger gown and Bella was looking like royalty in a black Zac Posen gown. They were in the box that overlooked the entire casino floor. There wasn't a spot in the casino that they couldn't see. The hotel was packed to capacity and they were booked full for the next six months! Everywhere you looked there was an A-lister.

"There go my girl Cardi B!" Kiki pointed.

"Act like you been somewhere," Bella said and they both laughed.

"We did it," Bella said.

"No, you did it. I really didn't do nothing"

"Like I said, we did it. We're equal partners. Everything is getting split down the middle."

"Come on, let's go work the room." Kiki pulled Bella out of the room.

Kiki had really let her hair down for this event. She'd had her long hair done in an updo with a strand of hair that fell on each side of her face. She had diamonds everywhere! Diamond earrings, diamond necklace, and diamond rings. She was so relaxed. She'd even left her guns in her suite upstairs.

The Mexican Cartel and OTF was so deep inside and outside the casino that if you did try anything, it would be the last thing tried.

"Bella, can we talk?" Chris walked up and grabbed her hand.

"Who the fuck are you? And you need to let her go," Kiki said.

"Bitch, mind your business!" he said.

"Why he say that?" Kiki was about to go stupid, but Bella put a hand on her arm.

"First off, Chris, this is my sister, and if you knew what I knew, you'd apologize."

"My bad, yo. I just really need to talk to your sister." he said.

"Chris? I heard that name before," Kiki said, racking her brain, trying to figure out where she'd heard the name from recently. "Oooohhh, this the little nigga Keishana said you gave your number to." Kiki looked him up and down.

"Little nigga?" Chris asked.

"If I said something wrong, why it ain't no blood in my mouth?" Kiki asked, mugging him. She was really feeling some type of way. In her mind, Bella was still Taz's bitch, so for another nigga to be in Bella's face, Kiki felt like it was her duty to defend Taz's honor.

"Chill, Kiki, I got this," Bella said.

"Nah, fuck that. She got me twisted with somebody else." Chris started to get mad.

"Since I got you twisted, all you got to do is act like you want smoke," Kiki whispered, trying to keep from making a scene.

"Come on, Chris." Bella pulled him away before Kiki punched him in his mouth.

Kiki watched as Bella locked her fingers with his as they walked away. She made a mental note to check Bella the first chance she got.

Kiki needed a drink. She went to the bar and sat on a stool. She got a double shot of gin and downed it.

"What's your name, gorgeous?"

"Not interested." she said, not turning around.

"You seem stressed. A little conversation with the right person might help." He wasn't giving up.

"And I suppose you're that person."

"Only one way to find out."

Kiki turned around to see who was pestering her and wasn't disappointed. He stood about 5'9" and was high yellow with waves. He was stocky, but not buff. The tuxedo he had on fit him perfectly.

"And who are you?" Kiki asked, looking at his lips.

"Tyrone. Tyrone Black." He extended his hand.

"Kiki." She shook his hand.

"So inform me as to why a pretty woman like you is at the bar by herself?" He licked his lips and Kiki's kitty jumped.

Kiki didn't know what was wrong with her. She was already feeling the effects of the gin since she hadn't eaten anything all day.

"This pretty woman is at the bar by herself because she wants to be. It's by choice."

"Well, do you mind if I join you?"

"It's a free country. You can do as you please."

"True, but I only want to be here if I'm wanted," he said, licking his lips again.

"Why do you keep licking your lips?"

"Because I keep imagining what you gon' taste like while you riding my face," he said, almost making Kiki choke on her drink.

As fast as the image came of her riding his face, it was gone. She was going to get on Bella about the same thing that she was thinking about.

"Nah, I got a man," she said, getting up and walking away.

"I been looking for you," Slick said, hobbling up on crutches.

"What does your crippled ass want?"

"So it's safe to say that South Carolina is mine, right? That way you'll have most of the Southern states under the OTF banner. You just have to let them niggas know they need to fall under me."

Slick had fallen back from Vinnie and was strictly dealing with Kiki.

"Don't make me regret this, Slick," Kiki stated. "But let me ask you this: who the fuck is supplying him?" she wanted to know.

"I honestly don't know. We've never discussed that."

Kiki needed to find this priceless information out and whoever it was had to be upper echelon because of the quality of their work.

"You're useless," she joked. "Get out my face."

"Hey Kiki." Erica walked up. "Slick, I need some more money."

"Let me go before this girl worry me to death." Slick hobbled away with his girlfriend.

Kiki spun in a circle, taking it all in. If she could get rid of Vinnie, a majority of her problems would be dealt with. Zeus and the Zoe Pound had just hit one of her spots in Miami, but the losses were minor. They'd be taken care of sooner rather than later. They weren't a major factor in her eyes. Bella said she had seen the Charger flip over the bridge and into the water, but he'd lived. He was luckier than Tom Brady in the Superbowl versus the Seahawks when they passed the ball instead of handing it off to Beast mode. It was okay though because Kiki was going to put the choppa to his head and pull the trigga. If he survived that, then he was meant to be on this earth.

Kiki shook hands and gave out hugs to most of the A-listers for the next two hours. She was exhausted! Kiki went to her suite and as soon as she kicked her heels off, she was out like a light.

Nicholas Lock

# Chapter 27

It was against her better judgement, but Kiki was taking Bella's advice and was going to take a backseat as far as putting in work. The first order she gave was for Flip to kill Agent Edwards. The task fell in his lap because Virginia was his responsibility and that's where Agent Edwards resided. He was taking three of his young guns with him. There was Jux, Jimmy, and Vega. They were ten years younger than him at nineteen and were the definition of ruthless. They all looked up to Flip. They even rocked their hair like Flip did. Vega was the only one who didn't. Flip had rented a black Dodge Durango for the task. Flip knew he had to make a statement with this one because he was trying to put on a good showing for Kiki.

It was nine at night when they pulled into the gated community that Edwards stayed in. Flip was hoping to catch him with his pants down. The plan was for Vega to go knock on the door and act as if he was selling candy. Vega was even dressed for the part. He had on a white collar shirt and some black slacks, the usual school uniform. Vega was the youngest-looking one. He had a fade and no facial hair. He could go for a kid in their early teens. But in actuality, he was the wildest one. They let him out with his box of candy that he'd bought from a kid that was really selling candy and he walked up to the door.

"Hi! I'm selling candy for my school. Would you like to purchase some?" he asked the lady who answered the door.

If she would've been thinking, she would've noticed it was too late for him to be out selling candy.

"Sure! Come on in while I get my purse."

The fox was in the henhouse. Vega followed her into the house. Once they got to the kitchen, he pulled his Beretta out and hit her in the back of her head, knocking her out. He tiptoed to the master bedroom and peeked in. The room was empty. He searched the rest of the house, and all he turned up was their teenage son and their niece who was visiting them from the University of Virginia. He caught them while they were unaware and tied them up. Flip, Jux, and Jimmy had come in while he was tying them up and tied up the wife. They moved everybody to the living room

"Please! Take what you want and leave!" the wife cried.

"Shut up!" Flip said. "Where's your husband?"

Jux slapped her across the face. "You're not going any motherfucking place until your husband shows up."

"Don't touch her again," her son growled.

They all looked at each other and laughed.

"Or what? You gon' do something about it?" Jux teased.

Jux slapped the boy's mom again, busting her lip.

"You cocksucker!" the boy screamed at Jux.

Jux walked over to the boy and untied him. "Now what you just call me?" Jux asked, handing his gun to Jimmy.

"Cocksucker," the boy said.

Jux swung on him, but he blocked it and connected with a jab that made Jux's nose start bleeding. Jux didn't know it, but he'd bitten off more than he could chew because Agent Edwards had put his son into boxing at an early age and at sixteen he was the Golden Glove runner-up. Jux rushed him and connected with a two piece. He ate them and hit Jux with an uppercut that put him on his ass.

"Boy, you better not let that white boy beat your ass!" Vega said.

Jux did what most niggas did when they started losing a fight: grab. Jux got to his feet and grabbed him.

"Oh shit, my nigga, you got to grab him?" Flip laughed.

Jux tried to jam the boy but ended up off his feet and onto the floor with the boy standing over him. Jimmy slapped the boy in the back of the head with his gun and he fell to the floor. Jux grabbed his gun and started pistol whipping him.

"Quit it!" his cousin screamed. "Oww!" she yelled as Vega snatched her by the ponytail.

"You'll get yours soon enough," he whispered in her ear, grabbing a handful of one of her breasts.

"A'ight!" Flip yelled, grabbing Jux's arm in mid-stroke. "Don't kill him yet."

Flip directed his gaze to the wife. "What's your name?"

"Madelyn. That's Courtney and my son David."

"Madelyn, you're going to call your husband and tell him to come home, that it's an emergency," Flip told her.

"Okay, just don't hurt us."

Flip untied her and let her call Agent Edwards.

"Damien, you need to come home now! I cut my pinky finger up really bad." She sobbed into the phone and hung up. "He's on the way."

"Well, while we wait…" Vega grabbed Courtney by her ponytail and dragged her down the hallway.

"Let me go!" She struggled against his hold.

He threw her into an office room and closed the door. He untied her and pulled the shirt she had been sleeping in over her head.

"Don't touch me!" she yelled, but it was all for nothing.

Vega punched her to the floor and then snatched her up. He ripped off the panties she had on and pushed her over the desk.

"No! Stop!" She tried fighting back, but received a closed fist for her efforts.

Vega pulled his dick out and entered her from behind. "Ughh," he growled.

"Hurry the fuck up!" Flip yelled peeking his head in the room. On the way back to the living room, Flip noticed a picture and something told him something wasn't right. He grabbed the picture and continued to the living room.

"Why was your husband dressed like this?" Flip pushed the picture into her face.

"He was graduating from West Point, the military academy!" she yelled.

He slapped her across the face with the pistol, breaking her nose.

"Fuck! Y'all get in here now!" he yelled, mad at himself.

Madelyn had played them. Flip didn't even know what her husband looked like. He'd just gotten the address from Kiki and rounded his young boys up without getting any more information. When Flip pushed the picture into her face, he'd had his hand on the bottom of the picture. The bottom read Cadet Colin Jacob Edwards, but on the phone she'd told Damian to come home.

"Who the fuck is Damian?" Flip yelled.

Jux, Vega, and Jimmy came back into the living room, throwing Courtney in the corner as something shattered the front window.

"What the fuck?" Jux yelled.

Jimmy was the unfortunate one that the object that flew through the window landed next to. BOOM! The flashbang grenade disoriented everyone except Flip. He was already halfway down the hallway when it went off. He'd gotten low as soon as the window shattered.

"Aaahhh!" Jimmy's whole right side was scorched by the blast of the grenade.

TAT! TAT! TAT!

Flip heard an assault rifle spit three times.

BOOM! BOOM! BOOM! One of Flip's young boys let their hammer go.

"Help me!" Jimmy continued to yell. He was in pain and he couldn't see.

Flip ducked into the office they'd had their way with Courtney in and closed the door. He opened the window, climbed out, and took off running to the Durango.

BOOM! BOOM!

TAT! TAT! TAT! TAT!

BOOM! BOOM! BOOM!

They were having an all-out shootout in the living room. Flip looked over his shoulder and saw the window lighting up from all the muzzle flashes. He got to the truck as the shots stopped. He got in and drove away. If one of them made it, they would understand.

Agent Edwards got the phone call from his wife while he was in his office looking over the file he had on Kiki and Isabella. When she'd called him Damian, he knew she was in trouble. When he'd started putting away the who's-who of the underworld, they'd discussed plans on what to do in certain situations. He knew there was a possibility that his family might get targeted in retaliation for some of his actions. The name Damian meant she was being held hostage and the pinky finger was her telling him there were four of them. Edwards immediately took off for his house. He went alone because he didn't want anyone poking around his house before he could straighten it out. Edwards had four hundred thousand dollars in his garage that he wouldn't be able to explain.

When he pulled into his neighborhood, he parked down the road and walked up to his house. He threw the flashbang in the window and came in through the garage. He took down three of the four intruders in less than five minutes. Edwards searched the house and couldn't find the fourth one. He got the lights on and saw that his son's body was riddled with bullets.

"Nooo!" his wife cried, seeing her son's lifeless body.

Edwards looked down and saw that the other bodies were black. Kiki was the first name that popped into his mind. He looked in the corner and saw his niece tied up and naked. He put his shirt over her and untied her.

"It's okay now," he soothed her.

*How did the fourth guy slip away?* he asked himself. He was going to make Kiki pay if it was the last thing he did.

\*\*\*

Justin was turning Alabama into his personal domain. With Kiki supplying him, he stamped that he was the king of Bama. He'd recruited forty members of the RUF, the Revolutionary United Front, from his hometown of Sierra Leone. They specialized in guerrilla warfare and back in the late 90's and early 2000's, they went toe to toe with Nigeria's military and local government.

There were only two older rebels and they were both thirty-five. Everyone else was younger than twenty-one. The youngest was only thirteen, but he was one of the deadliest. He had to be or he wouldn't survive. His name was Kio and he stood about 4'11" and was about 150 pounds. He'd gained almost forty pounds since coming from his poverty-stricken homeland.

Justin had taken over every major city in Alabama with Birmingham being his main resting place. With pure ruthlessness and savagery, the RUF took the cities by storm. The local dope boys weren't ready, nor were they equipped for the way the rebels attacked. In the end, it was get down or get laid down. Most of them chose to get down. That way they could keep their lives and continue to get money, which was a win-win.

Justin treated most of the white people he ran across in Alabama with absolutely no respect. He knew how black people were treated back in the day, from Rosa Parks to Martin Luther King Junior, so Justin was sure to return the favor. The rebels caught the attention of the big wigs.

Secretly, the governor and a few judges met with Justin and made a deal. If he could keep the violence to a minimum, he'd have free reign in Alabama, and of course he had to pay them a hundred G's a month. Justin agreed with a quickness. What he paid them a month he made in a week.

Kiki had called and requested that he and his crew cause a little ruckus for her and he planned to deliver. Flip and his team had botched a job and it was on Justin to fix it.

"I want this day to be etched in their memories for the rest of their lives," Justin said to the fifteen rebels he had with him. What they had planned was definitely out of the norm. All fifteen of the rebels were on Kawasaki 300's, two stroke dirt bikes, even Kio's little ass. Justin was on a Suzuki 450 four stroke. Today was the day of Agent Edward's son's funeral and Justin was getting ready to fuck it all the way up!

Agent Edwards and his wife had just sat down at the burial site when a bunch of dirt bikes crested the hill and sat there revving their engines. It was normal for the local kids to ride around on their dirt bikes, but they knew to stay away from the cemetery. By the time Edwards realized what was happening, the dirt by his feet started to kick up as bullets slammed into the dirt.

"Run!" he screamed as everything turned chaotic.

The police escorts attempted to fight back, but the rebels were too much. The dirt bikes were on them before they knew it. All Edwards was able to do was jump on top of his wife and cover her up.

"Ya! Ya! Ya! Ya!" the riders yelled.

While some of the riders harassed the people running, two of them rode up to the casket and hooked it up to their bikes. One of the riders couldn't have been any older than fourteen, but looking into his eyes chills run down Edwards's spine. His eyes had no emotion. It was like staring into two black holes.

"No, no, no!" he yelled when he saw what they were about to do. They revved their engines and took off, dragging the casket behind them. The lid popped open and David's body hung halfway out. There wasn't anything he could do but watch as they disappeared over the hill. He got up and saw his wife had a hole in the top of her head. She had been struck by one of the first bullets. He instantly blamed himself for not covering her up in time.

Agent Edwards had lost his son and wife in one week. His whole family was gone, all because of Kiki.

"You're dead!" he yelled. He'd never experienced pain like this. He was going to bury Kiki figuratively or literally, whichever one came first.

Nicholas Lock

# Chapter 28

Justin and the RUF rebels had made Kiki proud. After taking Agent Edward's son's body, they snuck into his house and laid him in his bed. Edwards had been avoiding his house because with his wife and son dead, it felt empty. The only time he went home was to wash and sleep. Other than that, he wasn't there. So when he started to notice the smell, it had been a few days. He went into his son's room and almost had a heart attack! His son's body had been put into the bed and was decomposing! Kiki was fucking him up mentally, which in turn was fucking him up physically. Agent Edwards broke down seeing his son's body. That was where they found him a week later, lying in the door to his son's room and crying. He was admitted to the psychiatric hospital, taking him out of Kiki's hair.

Kiki told herself she could get used to this. Calling shots from the comfort of her home was okay. And she wasn't done. Vinnie thought shit was sweet. He'd been sending teams to Baltimore, Fayetteville, ATL, and Miami. So far they'd been able to make a sizable dent in the OTF workforce, but she had endless supplies of soldiers. The news was trying to figure out why all these random acts of violence kept happening, but couldn't get a clear picture. The club massacre in Miami started the artery of gun control, then the assault of a federal agent in his home gave it gas. Then the agent's son's funeral was attacked, where his wife was killed and his son's body was stolen. The media had all kinds of far out stories with terrorists being the lead they were trying to run with. Well, Kiki was about to really give them a story because she'd sent Anthony and Akira to give Vinnie a wakeup call.

Obviously Vinnie really thought he was above and beyond because he had the audacity to have a public wedding for his daughter – a daughter no one knew he had. The only reason she'd found out was because she liked to read the wedding section in the newspaper. Kiki had a thing about weddings since she was a little girl but nobody knew it - nobody except Taz. He was the only one she ever let see that side of her. Kiki would always envision her and Taz in the wedding section. But that was neither here nor there. So she'd seen Vinnie in a picture with what said was his daughter and her fiancé and it was scheduled to take place Friday. And what a Friday it was going to be.

Anthony and Akira had heard about the how Justin had put on and now it was their turn. Anthony and Akira were just like Alex and Niko in the fact that they loved to put in work, more so Akira because as of late, Anthony was focused on getting money. They had piled into five black Ford Mustangs with Anthony and Akira in the front car. They got to New York the day before the wedding and got hotel rooms in New Jersey because they didn't want to be too close to where the action was going to take place. They'd brought eight of their homies with them. Everyone was dressed head to toe in clack and were strapped like the next World War was about to happen. If it was one thing Chicago niggas were good for, it was blowing that smoke!

"You know we about to put on, right?" Akira asked her older brother.

"Don't we always?"

"But this one has to be extravagant! I want to send the world a message that GD and OTF are not to be played with!" She pounded her fist into her hand.

Anthony got his lanky frame off the bed and put the blunt he was smoking into his sister's hand. She always worked herself up before putting in work and he'd always have to calm her down.

Anthony and Akira came from the typical black family: a broken home. Their father was nonexistent and their mother loved sucking on a stem more than she loved them. Anthony learned from an early age that he was going to have to not only fend for himself, but his little sister. Living on the Southside of Chicago, he had no choice but to be a lion. At ten years old, he'd caught his first body. He was selling crack and a crackhead tried robbing him. Anthony had a kitchen knife he kept hidden in his Starter jacket. He stabbed the head a dozen times and ran off. The next day, Anthony walked down the path and saw the crackhead was still lying there dead.

Anthony caught the eyes of one of the GD big homies and he took him under his wing. Gangster Disciples ran the section of the Southside that he lived on. They treated him like family, and they showed him love he wasn't getting at home. Akira looked up to him and whatever Anthony did, she did.

As Anthony rose through the ranks, his sister turned into a woman. At fourteen Akira had developed the body of a woman. She was stacked just like their mother was before crack had stolen her figure. Akira had a forty-inch ass and some 36C's. Anthony had threatened, shot, and beat up numerous niggas over his sister. Akira was the definition of beautiful and all the hustlers, gangbangers, and killers wanted to be the one to claim her as their own. She knew she was like that, but didn't flaunt it. She mostly wore clothes that were too big to try and hide her shape, but there was no hiding the body she had, plus her face belonged on the cover of a magazine. She put you in the mind of the late Aaliyah.

Anthony could still remember the day Akira got her introduction to the underworld. She had gone to a pajama party with some of her homegirls. It was one of the few times she dressed like a girl. She wore the pajamas she wore every night to bed, which was some silk pajama pants and top, but they were so tight you could see her pussy as clear as day. If Anthony would've been home, he would've made her change. She was having the time of her fifteen-year-old life. She was dancing with a nigga that couldn't keep his hands to himself, Akira didn't mind as long as he didn't get out of hand, plus he was twenty-three, and it felt good to be wanted by an older nigga. He'd been whispering sweet nothings in her ear the whole night and he convinced her to go in the back room with him. Akira had never had sex before. She'd fucked a few boys her age off and let a few of them eat her pussy, but she refused to suck their dick or let them enter her. They started kissing when they got into the room with him rubbing all over her ass. He was going to fuck her. He didn't give a fuck that she was jail bait.

"Mmm," Akira moaned as he sucked on her neck and toyed with her clit through her pajamas.

He slid her pajamas down and dived face first into her juice box. Akira was going to nut in his mouth and jack him off and go back to the party, but that game only worked on the boys her age, not grown men.

"Ah! Ah! Ahhh!" she yelled as her legs started to shake and she splashed her love juices all over his face.

He pulled his dick out of his balling shorts and got between her legs.

"Uh-uh." Akira scooted away and sat up. "Let me jack it."

"Jack it? Fuck that, I'm trying to fuck." He tried pushing her onto her back.

"No, I'm not about to fuck you. Maybe next time."

"You got me fucked up!" He snatched her by her hair and forced her onto the floor.

"No, get off me!" She fought back and he punched her, but that didn't stop Akira from fighting back.

Akira got to her feet and tried to run out of the room, but the dude grabbed her by her top and put her in the chokehold from the back. She clawed at his arms, but he was too strong. She felt herself about to black out when she reached behind her and got ahold of his nuts.

"Ahh!" he yelled, letting her go.

"You was going to rape me," she said, squeezing his nuts. Akira saw his razor had fallen out of his shorts pocket. She kept a firm hold onto his balls and bent to pick the razor up. When she came up, she brought the razor down as hard as she could, nearly severing his dick. It was only hanging on by a thin piece of meat.

"Aahh! Aahh!" he screamed looking down at his manhood.

"Shut the fuck up!" She slashed the razor across his neck, spraying herself with blood.

He fell to the floor on his knees, grabbing his throat as blood ran through his fingers.

"Fucking pussy!" Akira went into a rage, slashing him everywhere. Even after he was dead, she continued to go in.

They had to call Anthony to the party because she wouldn't let anyone come near her. When he got there, Akira was still in the room with the dead body with a smile on her face.

Anthony was able to get Akira back to the house and calmed down before their non-existent mother came home. He then went and dumped the body in the park. A dead body on the Southside of Chicago was nothing out of the ordinary, so there wasn't much of an investigation when the body was found.

From that day forth, she was as bloodthirsty as they came. All she understood was bloodshed. She did absolutely no arguing. She didn't even raise her voice for the most part.

Akira continued to let dudes eat her pussy but would never let them fuck her.

"After tomorrow, all our enemies are going to be on eggshells," Anthony said.

"You don't know the half." She pulled on the blunt he had passed her.

They laid back and mellowed out. Anthony fell asleep, but Akira was too wired up to sleep even with the weed in her system. When Anthony woke up the next day, Akira was still up smoking.

"Did you go to sleep?" He knew the answer.

She just shook her head. She was in her zone. He could tell because she wasn't talking. She was just fingering the Draco on her lap. Anthony shook his head and got dressed. They all filed out with one thing on their mind: murder.

On the ride to New York, Akira put Lil Durk's "Rumors" on repeat. They crossed the George Washington Bridge and everybody in all the cars cocked their weapons - everybody except Akira. Hers had been cocked since yesterday.

The Mustangs approached the church just as the bride and groom were making their way down the church steps.

CHA! CHA! CHA!

TAT! TAT!

KAH! KAH!

BOOM! BOOM! BOOM! BOOM!

They started letting their hammers talk immediately. Akira was out of the car before Anthony had a chance to stop. She had her sights on one person and one person only: Vinnie! Akira spotted his bodyguards roughly ushering him away.

"Nah, motherfucker!" she yelled, busting her gun at their backs.

Vinnie didn't give a damn about the bullets flying. He was trying to get to his daughter, but his bodyguards were forcing him to his limo.

BOOM! BOOM! CLICK! CLICK! Akira's clip ran out, so she pulled another thirty round. She took another clip out and slammed it into the Draco. BOOM! BOOM! BOOM! BOOM!

"Oh, y'all thought it was over!" she yelled, missing Vinnie, but hitting the bodyguard next to Vinnie, bathing him in blood. "Fuck!"

The bodyguards got Vinnie to his limo and pulled off. Akira ran behind the Lincoln MKZ limo shooting, but it was in vain because it was bulletproof. She ran back to the front of the church as the shooting stopped. Dead bodies littered the church steps.

"Help me!" a woman screamed as Akira was about to get in the Mustang.

"Come on, Akira!" her brother yelled as she made her way back to the church steps and saw that it was the bride yelling.

"Please help!" the bride screamed, cradling her husband.

"Come on, bitch!" Akira snatched her up, an idea popping into her head.

They peeled out, leaving behind pure mayhem. Among the dead was the Cardinal of New York, which was going to make the headlines worldwide. Also among the dead was the daughter of Vinnie's connect.

Nicholas Lock

# Chapter 29

Kiki fucked with Akira and her brother. They didn't get Vinnie, but they got his daughter. She couldn't have done much better herself. Once again, she was going to sit back and give orders.

Kiki had told Body it was time for him to show his teeth. She was leaving it to him to handle the situation with Vinnie's daughter. Kiki didn't want Anthony and Akira any hotter than what they were. With the Cardinal of New York getting killed, shit was super hot, especially since it was said he was next up to be the pope. Every news station in the world was talking about it, no matter what channel you turned to. Then coupled with the other major acts of violence, the President of the U.S. was talking about cracking down on violence. Niggas had to tread lightly.

Body had it set up to where Vinnie was going to meet him and exchange his daughter for a million dollars. But he wouldn't be leaving the meeting with his life or the money. Body had thrown the million dollars in to see if he could get an added bonus. Vinnie had agreed to meet in Kentucky. That way, Body would have the advantage plus Body wasn't going anywhere New York. Shit was way too hot up there.

Body had Vinnie coming to the outskirts of Louisville way out in the cut. There was an old park that sat off about two miles inside a wooded area. It was deserted, and the only people who frequented the park were the college students from the University of Louisville, and that was in the summertime. Even then, it was only the students who were attending summer classes or the few who chose not to go home for summer break.

But now it was the middle of December and snow had blanketed the ground.

"I don't want anybody to leave this meeting tonight but us," Body told his comrades.

They were twenty deep. Body set them up strategically around the park. A few were seen, but Body had others hidden. The people he had hidden had long range rifles and red beams. He was prepared for anything because Kiki had given him the rundown on Vinnie. He knew more than likely Vinnie was going to come deep and would have a trick up his sleeve.

"It's cold as hell!" Body blew into his hands.

His hands were the only thing bothering him. He had a black thermal over a T-shirt and the thermal was covered by a black and green Gucci jacket. His black Gucci jeans and construction Timberlands had his lower body warm. He thought about putting on some gloves, but then he wouldn't be able to grip the Taurus .45 like he wanted.

Off to the side and out of sight was a hole that was ten feet deep and seven feet long. After they killed Vinnie and whoever he brought along, they were going to bury them. A few feet away from that hole was where Body had buried the three niggas that were running Kentucky before him. This was his unofficial spot where he buried all his troubles.

It was a cold night like this one when Body had his big ass under Jamar's Denali. Jamar was one of the three niggas that had Kentucky under their thumb. There was Jamar, Mason, and Ethan. They were homeboys who ran Kentucky with an iron fist. Anybody who got money had to either cop from them or pay a tax. Body wasn't going for it, so he planned to knock them off and take the throne as King of Kentucky. It was hard to catch them all at the same spot at the same time, so Body had to improvise, which was the reason Body had his three hundred pound ass under Jamar's truck. Of the three, Jamar was the least cautious. He moved reckless and that night it would cost him dearly.

Jamar had come out of his house and got in the truck, but left the door open, giving Body the chance he needed. He rolled from under the truck and put his Desert Eagle in Jamar's face.

"Oh shit! Man, I ain't got nothing!" He threw his hands in the air.

"I ain't even asked you shit yet, nigga! This how it's going to go down. We about to go in your house and you're going to call Ethan and Mason over here." Body put the cannon to the side of his head.

"Okay! Okay, just don't shoot," he pleaded.

Body walked Jamar in the house and tied his legs together, but left his hands free so he could dial the numbers.

"Yo, Mason, I need you to swing by my house real quick. I think I got a power plug for us." Jamar convinced him to come through, then he called Ethan. "Bro, Mason already on the way to my spot. You need to swing through too so I can run this power plug by you too." He hung up. "They on the way."

Ethan got there first. Body opened the door with his Desert Eagle and forced him into the house before tying him up. Mason got the same treatment when he got to Jamar's house.

"You're making a huge mistake," Mason said.

Body laughed. "Maybe, but one thing about it, you won't live long enough to find out."

Body loaded them up into Jamar's Denali and drove them to the park in the cut where he had a ditch waiting for them. Instead of killing them beforehand, he buried them alive so they could suffer more.

"Here they come!" someone yelled.

Body saw headlights coming down the road and stepped out into the clearing. Seven cars and a Bentley Bentayga pulled in last. Vinnie got out of the first car followed by a bunch of his henchmen. Nobody got out of the Bentley SUV.

"Are you Body?" Vinnie asked.

"Yeah."

"Where's my daughter?"

Body gave a signal and two of his men brought Vinnie's daughter out to where they stood.

"Daddy!" she cried and tried to run to Vinnie, but Body's men held her beside them.

"Where's my money?"

Vinnie waved. The doors to the Bentayga opened up and three men emerged. One was carrying a suitcase and wearing a suit. This threw Body off because none of them were Italian. They looked like Arabs.

"And who the fuck are you?" Body asked.

"Benjamin Arafat."

"It doesn't even matter. Now where's my money?" Body was getting impatient.

The man in the suit who called himself Benjamin handed Body the suitcase he had in his hands. Body opened it and his dick got hard. The briefcase held bundles of blue-faced hundreds

"Let her go," he said and Vinnie's daughter rushed into his arms. "One more thing, Vinnie," Body said as Vinnie turned to leave.

"What, monkey?" Vinnie snapped.

"I need your life," he said as red beams danced around Vinnie's face.

BOOM! BOOM! BOOM! BOOM! BOOM!

A series of shots sounded off in the distance, but instead of Vinnie's men dropping it was Body's men.

"What the fuck?" Body said, turning around.

"It's obvious you're not up to date on current events," Benjamin Arafat said, stepping closer to Body "I'm the director of the Massad, the Israeli spy agency, the most powerful spy agency in the world. Yes, more powerful than the CIA. I have just as much power as the president of Israel, if not more. Now in the process of kidnapping Vinnie's daughter at her wedding, you killed mine." He let his words sink in as black-clad figures emerged from the spots Body had his men hidden. It was then that Body noticed the red dots were no longer on Vinnie, but on him.

It was ironic, Body thought to himself, that the same ground he used to bury his victims was now about to be his final resting place. But he wasn't going out like no pussy. He was going to die like the G he was.

"Fuck you and your daughter!" he yelled, pulling his Taurus.

Body didn't get a chance to raise his gun before his head exploded. The same hole that was supposed to hold Vinnie and his men was filled with Body and his men.

\*\*\*

"Why the fuck isn't Body answering his phone?" Kiki asked.

It had been three days since Body was supposed to meet Vinnie and kill him, but Kiki hadn't heard from him. She was starting to think maybe Vinnie had bested Body. Kiki tried to call Body again, and still didn't get an answer.

"Fuck!" She threw her phone across the room.

"What's the matter with you?" Travis asked.

"Body hasn't answered his phone in three days. I have to expect the worst. Come on, I need to take a ride."

Kiki, Travis, and two of her bodyguards walked out of her house and almost tripped on a package that was sitting on her porch.

"Anybody see who left this?" Kiki asked, picking the box up, and everybody shook their heads.

Kiki opened the box and looked inside. She couldn't do anything but laugh. Vinnie had taken a page out of her book and sent her Body's hands with a note. The reason she knew they were Body's was because he had *self-made* tattooed on his hands. Kiki grabbed the bloody note and read it. It said, "I want everybody's hands that had something to do with my daughter's death, but I want the head of the person who made the call." Kiki didn't understand because as far as she knew, Body hadn't killed Vinnie's daughter.

"Watch out! Watch out! Travis yelled, jumping on Kiki, knocking her to the ground.

Shots started to ring out. Her security converged on the shooters. It didn't take long for her security to handle the four shooters.

"Watch out, Travis!" Kiki tried to push him off, but he wouldn't move.

"Oh shit!" Kiki saw the blood coming out the corner of Travis's mouth.

Her security rolled Travis over and she knew from the glassy look his eyes held that he was dead. Kiki took one of the hammers off her security, made her way over to one of the dead shooters, and emptied the clip into his chest. Kiki bent down and snatched the ski mask he wore off and was confused. He wasn't Italian; he was Middle Eastern. Kiki went to the other three and they all looked Middle Eastern. Kiki's phone ringing snapped her out of her confusion.

"Yeah," she answered.

"Ms. Kiki, I understand your prowess. Next time instead of four, I'll send a hundred," a voice with a funny accent said.

"Who the fuck is this?"

"Someone you stole something very valuable from. And I intend to make you pay for it in the worst way possible," he said and then hung up.

Kiki went over her list of enemies in her head and couldn't come up with anybody that matched that voice. Little did she know this adversary would shake her world to the core.

Nicholas Lock

# Chapter 30

It was Christmas day and Bella and the kids had just gotten done opening their presents. But her mind was elsewhere. She was trying to figure out who the hell had Kiki in their sights other than Zeus, who she was sure had a higher power on his side because nobody dodged death like him. Then there was Vinnie, but Kiki had told her that the men who'd tried to kill her weren't Italians. Kiki said they looked like they were Middle Eastern, That was the part that was throwing her for a loop. Bella was exhausting all her resources and connections trying to figure out what was going on.

Then she had her own troubles to deal with. Her lawyer had told her that the FBI and DEA were snooping around and they had a confidential informant that said she was running the Mexican Cartel. Bella had made sure there were no connections between her and the Mexican Cartel. And she knew the informant definitely wasn't a Cartel member because they all knew that their family would pay the price. This was just somebody trying to get her out of the way. The more she thought about it, the more Bella knew that they had no case.

"Hello," she answered her phone.

"Merry Christmas, boo," Chris said.

Bella had been seeing Chris at a steady pace and he was starting to grow on her. He wasn't really her type because he wasn't a street nigga; he was a square. There was something different. But Bella still wanted that ruggedness in her man. His sex was the only thing that was saving him - that and the fact that he was a real sweetheart.

"What's up, Chris?"

"You don't sound too happy to hear from me," he said glumly.

That was another one of Bella's dislikes. Chris was sensitive as hell. Some women like men like that, but Bella wasn't one of them.

"It's not that. I just have a lot on my mind and a lot going on in my life right now," she said. Bella hadn't told him about her running the Cartel or her ties with OTF and she never would. He'd only been to her house one time and even then, he didn't come in. She'd made him stay in the car.

"If I was there, I'm sure I could ease your mind," Chris said, dropping his voice.

If there was one thing he was good at, it was eating pussy. The only person Bella knew that ate pussy better was Taz.

"You know that's not gonna happen, but I have to go by the casino later on to check on things. Maybe we'll meet up after that."

"Baby, when are you going to invite me into your house? And when am I going to meet your kids?"

"Listen, Chris, maybe I'll invite you over one day, but more likely than not it's not going to happen. You have to understand, my husband bought this house for us and the kids. And for me to have you in here would make me feel dirty. And Chris, there's not one legit reason I can come up with that would justify me introducing you to my children."

"So what, you don't see us having a future together?"

"Chris, I don't even know what's in my future," she said, getting irritated with his questions. "Let's just enjoy the moment, okay, and we'll see what happens. I'll call you when I get to the casino." Bella hung up not, giving him a chance to respond.

Bella went to get in the shower to see if she could wash some of the stress away before she started her day.

\*\*\*

Kiki needed to get out of Atlanta. She was beginning to feel closed in. Kiki, Meosha, Alex, and Tevin were driving to Miami to see what was going on. Alex had been doing his due diligence in Maryland, so much so that she'd given him Kentucky. Meosha must've been really putting it on him because she had him under her thumb. If Meosha said jump, Kiki was sure Alex would say how high. And Meosha had turned over a new leaf. She'd been Kiki's shoulder to lean on in times of crisis. This was how family was supposed to be, Kiki thought.

Kiki and Tevin were in her new yellow and black Audi R8 and Meosha and Alex were in Meosha's Porsche Cayenne truck.

"You sure you don't want to switch cars?" Kiki grinned.

"I'm good," he responded.

Tevin was 6'5" and close to three hundred pounds and he was driving Kiki's little-ass R8.

"We need to find out who this mystery man is because it's impossible to go on offense if you don't have anything to shoot at," Kiki said

"That's true. But don't worry about the defensive side of things. Playing defense is what I do for a living. You focus on putting this nigga in the dirt."

"Hopefully, Bella has found something out for me because I have nothing." She reclined her seat and put her arm across her eyes. Kiki now saw the shit Taz had to go through and why he stressed leaving the streets alone. If Kiki dealt strictly in her legit ventures, she would never have a stressful day. Everything would be peaches and cream. If she honestly felt like Meosha could lead OTF, Kiki would put it all on her shoulders, but with Meosha at the helm, OTF would sink to the bottom of the barrel. It reminded Kiki of a quote by

Publilius Syrus. He said anyone can hold the helm when the sea is calm. Meosha could run OTF if there wasn't a war going on with unknown parties because in time of conflict, her management skills were zero.

They got to Miami late in the afternoon. When they pulled up to the casino, things were starting to pick up. The casino floor was jam packed. While Meosha and Alex booked a room, Kiki went to go find Bella. After searching everywhere, she made her way to Bella's suite.

Kiki beat on Bella's door.

"I'm coming!" she heard Bella yell. "What's up, girl?" Bella asked, out of breath.

"Move, girl, and why are you out of breath?" She pushed Bella out of the way. Kiki went and plopped down on the couch. "Tell me you found something out for me."

"Not yet, but I have my people doing a check on all the girls that were killed that day to see who their fathers were. That way, we can narrow it down. Now bye, Kiki. I was in the middle of something."

Kiki looked at Bella's clothes and realized she had a man's shirt on. Kiki squinted her eyes and said, "Or was somebody in the middle of you?" Kiki got up and walked towards Bella's bedroom.

"Kiki, wait!"

Kiki walked into the bedroom and there in the middle of the bed was a naked Chris. Kiki whirled around and slapped Bella across the face. "You got Taz fucked up!"

"I'm going to give you that one, Kiki, but if you put your hands on me again, we gon' have a real problem," Bella warned.

"Whoa, whoa, everybody calm down." Chris came out in his boxers.

"Mind your business, little boy. This is way above your paygrade." Kiki cut her eyes at him.

"I'm about tired of your mouth." He moved towards Kiki.

"No, Chris!" Bella yelled, but it was too late.

Chris grabbed Kiki by her throat in an attempt to choke her, but Kiki caught his wrist and twisted it up.

"Aahh!" he screamed.

"Now tell me, Chris, which one do you want to lose: your life or your dick?" Kiki had her gun in her other hand, resting it on Chris's dick.

"Let him go, Kiki."

"Are you serious? If he'll put his hands on me, you don't think he'll put his hands on you? Furthermore, what happened to us not moving on to anybody else? Huh? Then to do it with this fuck nigga is a slap in Taz's face."

"It's not even that serious! We just be fucking. And how long am I supposed to keep my love life on hold, huh? I'm twenty-five years old! Am I supposed to die alone?"

Kiki couldn't believe her ears. Was this the same Bella that was willing to die for Taz? Was this the same Bella that had killed her own father because he'd killed Taz? On the other hand, Kiki could understand her frustrations because she'd almost felt weak a couple times herself, but she never went through with it. Kiki would always come to her senses. Kiki looked into Chris's eyes and saw a straight coward. How he'd gotten Bella, she'd never know. She lowered the gun and backed away.

"Fuck you, Bella." Kiki walked out.

Kiki was really feeling some type of way. She made her way downstairs and out of the casino. She started walking down the strip when Meosha pulled up beside her.

"Where you going, girl? Get in."

Kiki climbed into the backseat only to find Alex on the other side.

"Why you not in the front, nigga?" she asked. Then she saw the gun.

"Boy, point that shit somewhere else."

"Don't make me shoot you, Kiki. Hand me your gun," Alex said.

"What is this, some kind of joke?" Kiki looked to her twin.

"Give him the gun, Kiki, because he will shoot you," Meosha said, looking in the rearview mirror.

"What the fuck type of time y'all on?" Kiki asked, giving Alex her gun.

"Kiki, your run as the head of OTF is over. It's my turn. I was supposed to be the one running OTF. You just pop up after years of me being next in line and take my spot. All you had to do was let me lead and play the background, but your pride and ego is too big. Well, now you'll know how it feels, You're getting the short end of the stick," Meosha said.

"You've been holding this in all this time?" Kiki balled her face up. "I should've known you were a snake when you tricked Taz out the dick!" she spat. "And you, nigga! You got me thinking you let Niko get killed."

Alex smiled a baleful smile. "Nah, I didn't let him get killed. I killed him. Meosha showed me that he was dimming my shine and with him out the way, I could take off. Sure enough I got Maryland, Kentucky, and now we're going to run OTF."

"The power of pussy," Kiki mumbled under her breath.

"Say what?" Alex asked.

"I said y'all better kill me now, because if I get the chance, y'all is dead." She looked into Alex's eyes.

"Nah, we ain't gon' kill you. We got something way better than that," Alex said before sticking a syringe in her arm.

Kiki felt herself going out. She tried to reach for Alex, but the drug was already taking effect and he was easily able to swat her away. Kiki saw Alex's smiling face before she blacked out.

\*\*\*

Kiki hadn't been answering Bella's calls and the reason Bella was calling was of the utmost importance. Bella had made Chris leave after Kiki had stormed out. Kiki had Bella feeling bad about fucking with Chris, but Bella could see in Kiki's eyes that she kind of understand where Bella was coming from. She tried Kiki again, but still didn't get an answer. Bella needed to tell Kiki just who it was they were up against. Bella knew this man was like nobody they'd ever encountered. Bella was scared as to how things might turn out. The only person she felt like would be able to match him in his ruthlessness and intensify was Taz, and he was in the ground.

Bella went into the lobby looking for Kiki and ran into Tevin.

"Have you seen Kiki?" they asked each other.

"No, I thought she was with you," he said.

"She's not. Where's Meosha?"

"There she is right there." Tevin pointed.

"Have y'all seen Kiki?" Bella asked Meosha and Alex, and they both shook their heads no. "Meosha, I found out who it is that sent those shooters to Kiki's house. Benjamin Arafat's daughter was killed at Vinnie's daughter's wedding."

"Are you talking about that Israeli spy dude that went rogue?" Meosha asked.

"Yes," Bella said.

Benjamin Arafat had told Body that he was the director of the Massad, but he wasn't. He'd gotten fired and went the illegal route. He was now on the FBI's most wanted list. Everyone looked at each other because they all knew he was going to test their resolve to the fullest extent.

\*\*\*

Kiki woke up, but didn't immediately open her eyes. She was lying on something soft, but didn't know what. She could hear a familiar voice not too far away, but she couldn't place it.

Kiki opened her eyes and looked around. She was lying on a bed in what appeared to be a bedroom with a bathroom in it. She looked to her left and saw Vinnie looking at her with a smile on his face.

"My, my, Kiki. You've fallen on bad times," he said.

Kiki wobbled to her feet and tried to rush him, only to find that there was a glass wall that separated them.

"It's no use, my dear. You're my prisoner now. Alex hand delivered you to me. I would turn you over to my plug since you had his daughter killed, but I'd rather keep you here as my sex slave," he said, licking his lips.

"Fuck you!" Kiki beat on the glass.

"We'll see if you have that same attitude after a couple days with no food," he said and slid the wall back in place, hiding the secret room.

Kiki beat on the glass until her hands started to bleed, then she stumbled back to the bed and sat down. Reality started to set in when she realized there was nothing she could do. She'd been betrayed by those closest to her. Kiki knew she was going to die, but the tears didn't begin to fall until she began to think about how she'd never see her twins again.

# Epilogue

"It's time for you to go back now. I've done all that I can for you. The rest is up to you," she said.

"What? I just started back walking and you're kicking me to the curb?"

She laughed. "I saw you on the beach this morning doing burpees, so don't try to play me."

The hooded figure in her living room doorway just stood there staring at her.

"You don't scare me." She grinned.

"I'm not trying to."

"I know what it is you're scared of: two things. One, you don't know what you're going to find when you go back, and two, you're not sure whether or not you still have it," she said, hitting the nail on the head.

The hooded figure had been paralyzed and had only been walking for nine months. Little did they know she'd set up a test to see where they stood. On cue, the lights in the house went out and the front door was kicked in. Two masked men came in and one grabbed the woman up in a chokehold.

"Let me go!" she yelled.

The hooded figure moved like he had wings. They were at an advantage because they knew the layout of the house and the intruders did not.

"Ahhh!" one said, hitting his shin on the coffee table.

The hooded figure snatched him up. He grabbed the intruder's gun hand with one hand and chopped him in the throat, causing him to let go of the gun.

BOOM! BOOM! BOOM!

The intruder took three hollow points to the chest, killing him instantly. The other intruder shot at him and missed.

"Drop the gun or lose your life." The hooded figure had moved and had the gun to the back of his head.

He dropped the gun and still lost his life because the hooded figure blessed him with a dome shot. Two minutes later, the lights clicked on and she was standing there with a smile on her face.

"I knew you were ready. Bella and Kiki need you," Aunt D said. "Bella isn't ready for a real war. She can't even handle the Zoe Pound, so she's likely to get killed. And Kiki is missing."

The hooded figure was no longer hooded. The hood had fallen from around his head, showing that he rocked a Caesar. Hearing that Bella and Kiki were down bad was all he needed to hear.

"Get me a ticket to Miami ASAP," Taz said.

Zeus and Vinnie thought that Bella and Kiki were a problem, but now they were about to meet the closest thing to the devil.

**The End**

# Submission Guideline

Submit the first three chapters of your completed manuscript to ldpsubmissions@gmail.com, subject line: Your book's title. The manuscript must be in a .doc file and sent as an attachment. Document should be in Times New Roman, double spaced and in size 12 font. Also, provide your synopsis and full contact information. If sending multiple submissions, they must each be in a separate email.

Have a story but no way to send it electronically? You can still submit to LDP/Ca$h Presents. Send in the first three chapters, written or typed, of your completed manuscript to:

**LDP: Submissions Dept**
**Po Box 944**
**Stockbridge, Ga 30281**

*DO NOT send original manuscript. Must be a duplicate.*

Provide your synopsis and a cover letter containing your full contact information.

Thanks for considering LDP and Ca$h Presents.

Nicholas Lock

BOW DOWN TO MY GANGSTA

By **Ca$h**

TORN BETWEEN TWO

By **Coffee**

THE STREETS STAINED MY SOUL **II**

By **Marcellus Allen**

BLOOD OF A BOSS **VI**

SHADOWS OF THE GAME II

By **Askari**

LOYAL TO THE GAME **IV**

By **T.J. & Jelissa**

IF LOVING YOU IS WRONG... **III**

By **Jelissa**

TRUE SAVAGE **VIII**

MIDNIGHT CARTEL III

DOPE BOY MAGIC IV

CITY OF KINGZ II

By **Chris Green**

BLAST FOR ME **III**

A SAVAGE DOPEBOY III

CUTTHROAT MAFIA III

DUFFLE BAG CARTEL VI

By **Ghost**

A HUSTLER'S DECEIT III

KILL ZONE **II**

BAE BELONGS TO ME III

A DOPE BOY'S QUEEN III

By **Aryanna**

COKE KINGS V

KING OF THE TRAP II

By **T.J. Edwards**

GORILLAZ IN THE BAY V

3X KRAZY II

**De'Kari**

THE STREETS ARE CALLING II

**Duquie Wilson**

KINGPIN KILLAZ IV

STREET KINGS III

PAID IN BLOOD III

CARTEL KILLAZ IV

DOPE GODS III

**Hood Rich**

SINS OF A HUSTLA II

**ASAD**

KINGZ OF THE GAME VI

**Playa Ray**

SLAUGHTER GANG IV

RUTHLESS HEART IV

**By Willie Slaughter**

THE HEART OF A SAVAGE III

**By Jibril Williams**

FUK SHYT II

Nicholas Lock

By Blakk Diamond
TRAP QUEEN
By Troublesome
YAYO V
GHOST MOB II
Stilloan Robinson
KINGPIN DREAMS III
By Paper Boi Rari
CREAM II
By Yolanda Moore
SON OF A DOPE FIEND III
By Renta
FOREVER GANGSTA II
GLOCKS ON SATIN SHEETS III
By Adrian Dulan
LOYALTY AIN'T PROMISED III
By Keith Williams
THE PRICE YOU PAY FOR LOVE II
By Destiny Skai
I'M NOTHING WITHOUT HIS LOVE II
SINS OF A THUG II
By Monet Dragun
LIFE OF A SAVAGE IV
MURDA SEASON IV
GANGLAND CARTEL III
CHI'RAQ GANGSTAS II
By Romell Tukes

QUIET MONEY IV

THUG LIFE II

EXTENDED CLIP II

By **Trai'Quan**

THE STREETS MADE ME III

By **Larry D. Wright**

IF YOU CROSS ME ONCE II

ANGEL III

By **Anthony Fields**

FRIEND OR FOE III

By **Mimi**

SAVAGE STORMS II

By **Meesha**

BLOOD ON THE MONEY III

**By J-Blunt**

THE STREETS WILL NEVER CLOSE II

**By K'ajji**

NIGHTMARES OF A HUSTLA III

**By King Dream**

THE WIFEY I USED TO BE II

**By Nicole Goosby**

IN THE ARM OF HIS BOSS

**By Jamila**

MONEY, MURDER & MEMORIES II

**Malik D. Rice**

CONCRETE KILLAZ II

**By Kingpen**

Nicholas Lock

HARD AND RUTHLESS II
**By Von Wiley Hall**
LEVELS TO THIS SHYT II
**By Ah'Million**


**Available Now**


RESTRAINING ORDER **I & II**
By **CA$H & Coffee**
LOVE KNOWS NO BOUNDARIES **I II & III**
By **Coffee**
RAISED AS A GOON I, II, III & IV
BRED BY THE SLUMS I, II, III
BLAST FOR ME I & II
ROTTEN TO THE CORE I II III
A BRONX TALE I, II, III
DUFFLE BAG CARTEL I II III IV V
HEARTLESS GOON I II III IV
A SAVAGE DOPEBOY I II
HEARTLESS GOON I II III
DRUG LORDS I II III
CUTTHROAT MAFIA I II
By **Ghost**
LAY IT DOWN **I & II**
LAST OF A DYING BREED I II
BLOOD STAINS OF A SHOTTA I & II III

By **Jamaica**
LOYAL TO THE GAME I II III
LIFE OF SIN I, II III
By **TJ & Jelissa**
BLOODY COMMAS I & II
SKI MASK CARTEL I  II & III
KING OF NEW YORK I II,III IV V
RISE TO POWER I II III
COKE KINGS I II III IV
BORN HEARTLESS I II III IV
KING OF THE TRAP
By **T.J. Edwards**
IF LOVING HIM IS WRONG…I & II
LOVE ME EVEN WHEN IT HURTS I II III
By **Jelissa**
WHEN THE STREETS CLAP BACK I & II III
THE HEART OF A SAVAGE I II
By **Jibril Williams**
A DISTINGUISHED THUG STOLE MY HEART I II & III
LOVE SHOULDN'T HURT I II III IV
RENEGADE BOYS I II III IV
PAID IN KARMA I II III
SAVAGE STORMS
By **Meesha**
A GANGSTER'S CODE I &, II III
A GANGSTER'S SYN I II III
THE SAVAGE LIFE I II III

Nicholas Lock

CHAINED TO THE STREETS I II III
BLOOD ON THE MONEY I II
**By J-Blunt**
PUSH IT TO THE LIMIT
By **Bre' Hayes**
BLOOD OF A BOSS **I, II, III, IV, V**
SHADOWS OF THE GAME
By **Askari**
THE STREETS BLEED MURDER **I, II & III**
THE HEART OF A GANGSTA I II& III
By **Jerry Jackson**
CUM FOR ME I II III IV V VI
An **LDP Erotica Collaboration**
BRIDE OF A HUSTLA **I  II & II**
THE FETTI GIRLS **I, II& III**
CORRUPTED BY A GANGSTA I, II III, IV
BLINDED BY HIS LOVE
THE PRICE YOU PAY FOR LOVE
DOPE GIRL MAGIC I II III
By **Destiny Skai**
WHEN A GOOD GIRL GOES BAD
By **Adrienne**
THE COST OF LOYALTY I II III
**By Kweli**
A GANGSTER'S REVENGE **I II III & IV**
THE BOSS MAN'S DAUGHTERS I II III IV V
A SAVAGE LOVE  **I & II**

212

BAE BELONGS TO ME I II

A HUSTLER'S DECEIT I, II, III

WHAT BAD BITCHES DO I, II, III

SOUL OF A MONSTER I II III

KILL ZONE

A DOPE BOY'S QUEEN I II

By **Aryanna**

A KINGPIN'S AMBITON

A KINGPIN'S AMBITION **II**

I MURDER FOR THE DOUGH

By **Ambitious**

TRUE SAVAGE I II III IV V VI VII

DOPE BOY MAGIC I, II, III

MIDNIGHT CARTEL I II

CITY OF KINGZ

By **Chris Green**

A DOPEBOY'S PRAYER

By **Eddie "Wolf" Lee**

THE KING CARTEL **I, II & III**

By **Frank Gresham**

THESE NIGGAS AIN'T LOYAL **I, II & III**

By **Nikki Tee**

GANGSTA SHYT **I II &III**

By **CATO**

THE ULTIMATE BETRAYAL

By **Phoenix**

BOSS'N UP **I , II & III**

Nicholas Lock

By **Royal Nicole**
I LOVE YOU TO DEATH
**By Destiny J**
I RIDE FOR MY HITTA
I STILL RIDE FOR MY HITTA
By **Misty Holt**
LOVE & CHASIN' PAPER
By **Qay Crockett**
TO DIE IN VAIN
SINS OF A HUSTLA
By **ASAD**
BROOKLYN HUSTLAZ
By **Boogsy Morina**
BROOKLYN ON LOCK I & II
By **Sonovia**
GANGSTA CITY
By **Teddy Duke**
A DRUG KING AND HIS DIAMOND I & II III
A DOPEMAN'S RICHES
HER MAN, MINE'S TOO I, II
CASH MONEY HO'S
THE WIFEY I USED TO BE
**By Nicole Goosby**
TRAPHOUSE KING **I II & III**
KINGPIN KILLAZ I II III
STREET KINGS I II
PAID IN BLOOD **I II**

CARTEL KILLAZ I II III

DOPE GODS I II

By **Hood Rich**

LIPSTICK KILLAH **I, II, III**

CRIME OF PASSION I II & III

FRIEND OR FOE I II

By **Mimi**

STEADY MOBBN' **I, II, III**

THE STREETS STAINED MY SOUL

By **Marcellus Allen**

WHO SHOT YA **I, II, III**

SON OF A DOPE FIEND I II

**Renta**

GORILLAZ IN THE BAY **I II III IV**

TEARS OF A GANGSTA I II

3X KRAZY

**DE'KARI**

TRIGGADALE I II III

**Elijah R. Freeman**

GOD BLESS THE TRAPPERS I, II, III

THESE SCANDALOUS STREETS I, II, III

FEAR MY GANGSTA I, II, III IV, V

THESE STREETS DON'T LOVE NOBODY I, II

BURY ME A G I, II, III, IV, V

A GANGSTA'S EMPIRE I, II, III, IV

THE DOPEMAN'S BODYGAURD I II

THE REALEST KILLAZ I II III

**Tranay Adams**

THE STREETS ARE CALLING

**Duquie Wilson**

MARRIED TO A BOSS... I II III

**By Destiny Skai & Chris Green**

KINGZ OF THE GAME I II III IV V

**Playa Ray**

SLAUGHTER GANG I II III

RUTHLESS HEART I II III

**By Willie Slaughter**

FUK SHYT

**By Blakk Diamond**

DON'T F#CK WITH MY HEART I II

**By Linnea**

ADDICTED TO THE DRAMA I II III

IN THE ARM OF HIS BOSS II

**By Jamila**

YAYO I II III IV

A SHOOTER'S AMBITION I II

**By S. Allen**

TRAP GOD I II III

**By Troublesome**

FOREVER GANGSTA

GLOCKS ON SATIN SHEETS I II

**By Adrian Dulan**

TOE TAGZ I II III

LEVELS TO THIS SHYT

**By Ah'Million**

KINGPIN DREAMS  I II

**By Paper Boi Rari**

CONFESSIONS OF A GANGSTA I II III

**By Nicholas Lock**

I'M NOTHING WITHOUT HIS LOVE

SINS OF A THUG

**By Monet Dragun**

CAUGHT UP IN THE LIFE I II III

**By Robert Baptiste**

NEW TO MONEY, MURDER & MEMORIES

THE GAME I II III

By **Malik D. Rice**

LIFE OF A SAVAGE I II III

A GANGSTA'S QUR'AN I II III

MURDA SEASON I II III

GANGLAND CARTEL I II

CHI'RAQ GANGSTAS

By **Romell Tukes**

LOYALTY AIN'T PROMISED I II

**By Keith Williams**

QUIET MONEY I II III

THUG LIFE

EXTENDED CLIP

By **Trai'Quan**

THE STREETS MADE ME I II

By **Larry D. Wright**

Nicholas Lock


THE ULTIMATE SACRIFICE I, II, III, IV, V, VI
KHADIFI
IF YOU CROSS ME ONCE
ANGEL I II
By **Anthony Fields**
THE LIFE OF A HOOD STAR
By **Ca$h & Rashia Wilson**
THE STREETS WILL NEVER CLOSE
By **K'ajji**
CREAM
By **Yolanda Moore**
NIGHTMARES OF A HUSTLA I II
By **King Dream**
CONCRETE KILLAZ
By **Kingpen**
HARD AND RUTHLESS
By **Von Wiley Hall**
GHOST MOB II
**Stilloan Robinson**

**BOOKS BY LDP'S CEO, CA$H**

TRUST IN NO MAN

TRUST IN NO MAN 2

TRUST IN NO MAN 3

BONDED BY BLOOD

SHORTY GOT A THUG

THUGS CRY

THUGS CRY 2

THUGS CRY 3

TRUST NO BITCH

TRUST NO BITCH 2

TRUST NO BITCH 3

TIL MY CASKET DROPS

RESTRAINING ORDER

RESTRAINING ORDER 2

IN LOVE WITH A CONVICT

LIFE OF A HOOD STAR

Nicholas Lock